FOLKTALES FROM THE
IRISH COUNTRYSIDE

FOLKTALES
FROM THE
IRISH COUNTRYSIDE

KEVIN DANAHER

MERCIER PRESS

MERCIER PRESS
PO Box 5, 5 French Church Street, Cork
16 Hume Street, Dublin 2

Trade enquiries to CMD DISTRIBUTION,
55a Spruce Avenue, Stillorgan Industrial Park, Blackrock, Dublin

First published in 1967, this edition 1998
© Kevin Danaher

ISBN 0 85342 849 2

18 17 16 15 14 13 12 11

In memory of my first and best storyteller
– My Father

Printed in Ireland by Colour Books Ltd.

Contents

INTRODUCTION

With a whole generation of young people growing up who cannot remember a time when there was no television, and whose parents cannot remember a time when there was no radio and no cinema, it is not surprising that many of them wonder what on earth people in country places found to do with their time in the winter evenings long ago. They find it difficult to understand that even the longest winter evening, stretching into the small hours of the morning, was too short for the entertainment which people were able to provide for themselves in the past, with singing, music and dancing, with cards and indoor games, with good talk and discussion around the fire, with *seanchas* and storytelling.

Not, of course, that all these diversions were afoot on the same evening or in the same house. But in every country parish and village it was known that there was always the chance of a game of cards in one house, that there was sure to be a bit of music in another, that the children would be playing 'Jack is alive' or 'Hide and go seek' in another, and that there were certain houses where a few of the older people would gather to 'draw down old times' and entertain the company with traditions of former days and with stories handed down by word of mouth from a past so distant that the scholars of today can only guess at its remoteness.

A part of our destiny in this changing world seems to be that every advance in technology and science still further reduces the self-sufficiency which was a characteristic of the rural communities of the past. We depend more and more upon the delivery van, the chain store, the mechanic and the technical expert to supply needs which in the old days were filled directly by the farmer, the housewife and the country craftsman. The same is true of recreation and pastime; for these we depend more and more upon the modern mass media of information and entertainment, on radio, television and cinema, on glossy periodicals and paperback novels. Our forefathers had none of these, even the printed word was scarce, for the library of the average farmhouse consisted of little more than a few school books, together with *Old Moore's Almanac* and a couple of prayer books. They had to provide their own entertainment, and at this they were very good. Indeed, the individual who could not contribute something to an evening's entertainment, who could not sing a song or tell a story, was regarded as a lesser being, one who, as far as the company was concerned, could have stayed at home for himself and not have gone visiting a neighbour's house at all. This very point is emphasised in the first story in this collection.

When I was a child in County Limerick in the 1920s, the ancient art of storytelling was already dying out. But there still were old people who knew the old stories, and although they seldom could claim an audience around the winter fire such as they themselves had known when they heard the tales from their old people 50 or 60 years earlier, they were always ready to heed a child's request for a story, and they provided us with many happy hours of wonder and of laughter. In the following pages I have tried to set down some of their stories as I remember them being told, in the hope that they may give pleasure to others.

The tales given below come from six different sources, all from County Limerick. Four of the storytellers were near neighbours of our own in the parish of Athea. The first of these was an elderly farmer named Thomas Moran, of Parkana, a broad-shouldered thick-set man who had been noted for his strength in his younger days and was still ready to do a day's farm work with the best of the younger men. He was very fond of children and always yielded to our demands for stories. He loved to tell of ghosts and fairies and monsters, which made us shiver delightedly in our shoes. He frequently tried to dispel our fears, although his reassurances were often as alarming as his tales, as when, in response to the question, was he not afraid to go into the haunted house, he came back with, 'In dread, is it? What would I be in dread of, and the souls of my own dead as thick as bees around me?'

His next door neighbour, Mrs Kate Ahern, was the second

of our storytellers. She was known in the whole district as a woman of great piety and of boundless charity, so much so that her daughters were often annoyed by the number of callers at her door, some of them asking for her prayers, others seeking more material help in money or kind. Never was she known to refuse a kind word or a helping hand to the distressed. Many people held that she was a saint, and that Heaven never refused her prayers; it was told that an irreverent fellow on being warned by the priest that he should pray for grace, replied that 'them people up above have no time to listen to anyone until all Kate Ahern's prayers are answered'. But for all her piety she was no gloomy puritan, for she loved humour and gaiety and music; at 70 years of age her walk was still as light as that of a young girl, and she was still ready to show the younger people how the intricate steps of a jig or a reel should be performed. She loved to listen to songs and music on her gramophone, and when some straight-laced killjoy averred that the gramophone was an instrument of the devil, she squashed him with the remark: 'Well, if he is inside in it, he is a right good fiddle player!' Her tales were mostly of the moral kind, of good deeds rewarded, of the virtues and miracles of the saints and of the mercy of God.

The third of our storytellers, Richard Denihan, whom we used to call 'Old Dick' to distinguish him from his son 'Young Dick', had been a parish priest's servant and general factotum in his younger days. He was very neat and handy and had great skill and knowledge in gardening; he often came to our house to do some gardening for my mother, and much of his time, I fear, was taken up by our pestering him for stories of the 'old times'. He had always an enquiring mind and a very retentive memory, which made him a veritable mine of information about the traditions of the past.

Our fourth, John Herbert, lived about three miles away, but had a married daughter who was a near neighbour of ours, and so we met him from time to time. He was a famous mower with the scythe – it was said that he could, in his time, cut an Irish acre a day, and that was much more than the average man could do – and also an expert thatcher. In pursuit of these trades he had travelled far and wide, and was often out very late at night or very early in the morning; many of his stories were about ghosts and other strange beings encountered on his travels.

Seven of the stories in this collection come from my own family. As a child my father had lived for some years with his grandmother, a farmer's widow, in the middle of County Limerick. Her maiden name was Mary Culhane, daughter of Thomas Culhane of Riddlestown, a prosperous farmer. She was born in 1798 and had a better schooling than the average country girl of the time, as she had attended a dame's school conducted by two ladies named the Misses Peppard in Rathkeale. She was bilingual, speaking both Irish and English with great ease, and was especially skilful in rapid translation from either language to the other. She could, in fact, take up a book or paper printed in English and read out the translation without pause. One of her grandson's memories recalls this talent: 'During the last year I spent in Ballyallinan I remember how my grandmother brought from Rathkeale a bundle of newspapers, included in which was a copy of the *Illustrated London News* in which was set forth with copious pictures a detailed account of the 'Invincibles' and their deeds. One of these – Joe Brady – was known locally, as he had worked as a stone-cutter at Rathkeale church in 1871. Well, indeed, I remember how I stood on tiptoe between the two old women as my grandmother told the story in vivid Irish while the pictures passed before our eyes. In after years, as a teacher, I often thought of that picture lesson.'

I have no doubt that my great-grandmother used this gift of rapid translation to supplement her own store of traditional tales with others culled from written sources. The versions of her stories given here are from my father's retelling of them, he having heard them in Irish from the old woman. But in the year 1883, when he was nine years old and living with his grandmother, there began to be published a weekly magazine, *The Irish Fireside*, selling at one penny per issue, and the earlier numbers of this periodical (July to November, 1883) carried a series of tales under the general title 'Irish Folk Lore'. The resemblance between certain of these and some of the old lady's tales recounted in Irish is close enough at least to suggest that – although my father did not say so definitely – she translated the written version for her circle of listeners.

When visiting my mother's people in the eastern part of County Limerick, in the Kilfinane district, we made the acquaintance of the last of our storytellers, a farm labourer named Michael Dawson who used to work for some of our cousins and was known as a good teller of tales. He had a serious, rather ponderous style of delivery and liked to give the magical and horrible aspects of his stories their full value. Some of his tales, he informed us, he had learned from his wife who was from the district of Rathmore in south-east County Kerry. I visited Mike Dawson again in the year 1940 and took down some of his tales with the help of a dictating machine; some of these were printed in *Béaloideas*, vol. xvii. The versions given in this present collection, however, like all the others included here, are culled from my memory of his first telling of them to us.

The ancient art of storytelling is rapidly dying out in Ireland. There are, indeed, remote corners of the land where a handful of old people survive who can still recount the old tales in the old way, but few of them can now gather an audience appreciative of their stories. The voice which now claims attention in the chimney corner is the mechanical one emanating from a shiny electrical apparatus, and I doubt if there is a single storyteller of the old style left in County Limerick today. Those who told us these and many other stories 40 years ago are all now gone to their reward. If there is storytelling in Heaven I can imagine them recounting their tales to admiring circles of junior angels, Mrs Kate Ahern to the manner born and very much at home in that celestial company, Tom Moran with a sly glance under bushy eyebrows to see if he can take a 'rise' out of some guileless cherub. Of this I am sure – that a Heaven without good storytelling is not truly Heaven for these old friends.

STORIES FROM TOM MORAN

1: The Boy who had no Story

There was a young fellow from this parish long ago, and it was always said that there was no great welcome before him in the house where he would go of an evening, because you might as well have a rock of bogdeal stuck up in the corner as to have himself, for he was dumb in any sort of entertainment, without a song or a story or even a handful of riddles in his head.

He used to travel away down the County Limerick, working for the farmers, and he used to put up here and there along the road, and before long he noticed that he was not very welcome, for although the people were hospitable to the stranger, they expected him to have all the latest news or to keep the night going with a song or a story. Poor Paddy was heart-scalded, but what could he do, the poor fellow?

Well, one night he was going along a lonely part of the road, and he saw this light in a house away inside in the fields, and he made for it. It was a queer, dark, big-looking house, and the door was opened by a queer, dark, big-looking man. 'Welcome, Paddy Ahern,' says the man. 'Come on in and take a seat at the fire.' Paddy could not make out how the man knew his name, but he was too much in dread to say anything, for it was a very queer place. They had the supper, and the man showed Paddy where to sleep, and he stretched himself out, tired after the road.

But it was not much rest he got. He was hardly asleep when the door burst open, and in with three men and they dragging a coffin after them. There was no sign of the man of the house.

'Who will help us to carry the coffin?' says the first of the men to the other two.

'Who but Paddy Ahern?' says they.

Poor Paddy had to get up and throw on his clothes, and he was shaking with the fright. He had to go under the feet of the coffin with one of the men, and the other two went under the head. Off with them out the door and away across the fields. It was not long until poor Paddy was all wet and dirty from falling into dykes and all torn and scratched from pulling through hedges and ditches. Every time he stopped they abused him, and a few times he fell they held kicking him until he got up again. He was in a terrible way. Finally they came to a graveyard, a frightful lonesome looking place with a high wall around it.

'Who will take the coffin in over the wall?' says the first man.

'Who but Paddy Ahern?' says they.

Poor Paddy had to lift the coffin in over the wall, although it nearly bested him. He was hardly able to stand by this time. But they would not let him take a rest.

'Who will dig the grave?' says the first man.

'Who will dig it but Paddy Ahern?' says they.

They gave him a spade and a shovel, and made him dig the grave.

'Who will open the coffin?' says the first man.

'Who will open it but Paddy Ahern?' says the other two.

He was nearly fainting with the terror, but he had to go down on his knee and take off the screws and lift the cover. And do you know what? The coffin was empty, although it was a frightful weight to carry.

'Who will go in the coffin?' says the first man.

'Who will go in it but Paddy Ahern?' says they.

They made a drive for poor Paddy, but if they did, he did not wait for them, but away out with him over the wall in one leap, and away across the country, and the three after him with every screech out of them and every halloo, the same as if it was the hunt. They nearly had him caught more than once, but he managed to keep out in front of them, until he saw a light in a window. He made for it and he shouting at the top of his voice to the people of the house to come and save him. But who should open the door, but the queer, dark, big-looking man. That was too much for poor Paddy; he fell in around the kitchen in a dead faint.

When he recovered his senses, it was broad daylight, and the queer man was up and working around the kitchen. There was not a sign of anyone else in the house.

'You are awake Paddy,' says the man of the house. 'Did you have a good night's sleep?'

'*Go bhfóiridh Dia orainn*,' says poor Paddy, 'but I did not. It is destroyed I am after all the hardship I had to put up with during the night! And not one single minute longer will I stay in this house, but to be legging it away as quick as I can!'

He got up and put on his clothes, and would you believe it? There was no sign of the night's hardship on them. They were his old working clothes, of course, but they were clean enough and dry. He did not know what to make of it.

'Now, listen to me, Paddy Ahern,' says the man of the house. 'It was how I was sorry for the way you were going the road, without a story or a song in your head. But tell me this much now – haven't you a fine adventure story to be telling in every house you go to, after last night?'

Not a word out of poor Paddy, but to grab up his stick and his bundle and away with him as quick as his legs could carry him. And whatever look he gave back and he crossing the ditch to the main road, there was not a house nor a sign of one to be seen but only the bare fields and a few cows grazing on them.

2: *The Spinning Woman*

It was all spinning and weaving long ago to make every kind of clothes and every kind of a cloth that would be wanted for the house. Shirts and sheets and things like that – they used to make them out of linen, and the clothes that the men and the women had, it was out of wool they were made. And there were poor women and the way of living they had was spinning the flax or the wool, and the people would bring them the carded flax and the carded wool and they would spin the thread. And the most of them were very good and they had plenty to do. When they had the thread spun and rolled up in big balls, they would weigh it, and it was according to the weight they were paid, and according as the thread was coarse or fine. Of

14

course there was a lot more spinning in a pound of fine thread than there would be in a pound of coarse thread.

Well, there was a little widow-woman living in a little one-roomed house over in Binn a' Ghleanna, and that was her way of living. And she was a great hand to spin any kind of thread and she got plenty to do. Boasting they used to be that the thread for the new suit was spun by her. And there was another thing that she was famous for in all the seven parishes around, and that was for helping women in labour. It was well known that there was no fear that anything would happen the woman or the infant that she would attend.

It happened one night that she was spinning away and she alone in her little house. And the knock came to the door, and it was a woman she never saw before, and a call to come to help a woman in childbirth. And she did not care much for going, and all the wool to be spun, and it belonging to a neighbouring farmer's wife that was a good customer. But the woman at the door begged her to come on. 'And I'm telling you that you won't be the worse for it,' says she. So off she went.

What surprised her was that there wasn't any sort of a car or a conveyance outside the door for her, for it was always the way that a trap or a side car, or at least a common car was to be sent for the midwife. But this night there was no car. And what surprised her more was that the woman brought her across the fields and not on the road at all. And it seemed to her that there were paths across the fields where she never before saw a path, and gaps and steps across the ditches where she was sure they were never before, and in no time at all where were they but down at the fort over in Jack Dan's place. And a door opened in the side of the fort, and the woman took her hand and brought her in. And faith! she had no time to be frightened, for there was a handsome young woman there in the bed, and she in labour, and the widow-woman only threw off her shawl and went to help her, and it wasn't long until the loveliest infant you ever saw was born. And the woman that brought her took her by the hand again, and in no time at all they were back at her own little house.

But the minute she went inside the door, what did she see

but every bit of the wool spun into the finest thread, and the little woman from the fort said to her, 'What did I tell you? All you have to do from this out is to leave the wool that is over after your day's spinning alongside the spinning wheel, and it will be all done in the morning. But take good care that you never tell the secret to a living soul,' says she. And with that she was out the door and away, and the widow-woman never saw her again. And now she was more famous than ever for the fine thread she made. And a queer thing happened, for there was another poor woman in the same way of living, and she asked her to give her a hand. And the other woman brought her wool for the widow-woman to spin for her. And she left it alongside the wheel with her own wool, and in the morning her own wool was done, but the other woman's wool was not touched.

3: *The Buried Treasure*

It is many a thing is buried in the ground that the people walking across it know nothing about. I suppose I walked through that field at the back of the Blessed Well over in Templeathea twenty times if I did it once, and it was a great scalding to my mind to know that there was the skin of a cow and it full of gold and treasures buried in the field, and I not knowing where to look for it. It is there yet. It was the monks from the old church that hid it, and no one knows where it is. It was in the bad times when the English were paying five pounds to anyone that brought them the head of a priest or a monk, and five pounds was a lot of money in those times. I do not know how they could tell the head of a priest or a monk from the head of an ordinary man, and I suppose they were often cheated by people who did up anyone's head to look a bit holy, for the man that would sell a monk's head would think nothing of roguery of that kind.

Well, anyhow, the English soldiers were coming, and there were those with them that would point out the priest or the monk for the price of a noggin of whiskey without talking about five pounds. The word was sent to the monks, that it was time for them to be moving to a safer place, and they went away. But before they went they took what valuables they had – I suppose they had not much money, but they had a lot of beautiful gold crosses and chalices in the church – and made a bundle of them inside the skin of a cow and buried it in the field at the back of the church. And by that time the soldiers were in the mouth of the road to them, and they had to run. And they never came back, or sent any word of where the gold is.

I heard tell that many is the one went to look for it. There was one man digging away and his spade hit against something soft with something hard inside in it. 'I have it!' says he. And the next thing was that he felt the hot breath on the back of his neck. And when he turned around, there was this big black bull looking in between his two eyes. I tell you he was not long leaving the field. And he would not even go back for his spade; he sent a *garsún* for it the day after.

A worse thing happened to a man from behind in Doirín. Maybe it was how he heard about the other man that found the soft thing with the hard thing inside in it, but anyhow he went digging along with his two sons. And they could see the house from where they were digging and it was about a mile and a half away. And the mother told the boys that she would put her white apron up on the bush and when they saw it they were to come home because the supper would be ready for them. And they had every second eye on the house, and the next thing was they saw this big cloud of smoke. *'Grádh Dé ináirde*! The house is burned!' says the boy and off with him, running, off with the father and the other boy after him. When they got down to the Glin road they looked again and there was the house and the sun shining on it and not a sign of fire. Back they went to the digging. And the other boy gave an eye to the house, and he sees this big *bladhm* of flames rising from it. Away with them again, until they were only three fields from it, and there it was and not a sign of fire on it.

'Look here, lads,' says the old man. 'It is our eyes it is, and we won't take any more notice of it.'

Well and good, back they went, and sure enough it was not

long until they saw the smoke and the flames again. And they took no notice but kept on digging for the gold. And after a while, the young lad says: 'There's my mother and she running around the house, screeching. And there are the neighbours and they all running with buckets and every sort of thing.'

'It is in your eyes, I tell you!' says the old man.

But the young lad was frightened and he began to cry, and the brother said he'd go home with him. And the father had to give in and come home too. And when they came to the house they found it burned to the ground. And it was the price of them when they would not take the first warning or the second one. It was too avaricious they were.

4: *The Three Wishes*

The old people always used to say that saints and holy people were going the road long ago, and that you should never refuse an alms to a poor person, for fear it would be an angel or Our Lord Himself asking for it. Well, there was a poor man living somewhere down in the County Limerick and he was working for a big farmer. And indeed he was better off than a lot of people with his constant work and the *bothán* and the quarter of ground free from the farmer, and it isn't everyone had that much in the old times, but that did not stop him from complaining about how poor he was. What was wrong with him was that he had no hold at all of the pence, and his wife, God help us, was a bit of a *straoil*, not a bit handy about the house and no good to spare a halfpenny, and so it often happened that they were without the next bite of food or the next sod of turf for the fire. But they were not a bit mean, and when any poor person came to the door asking for alms they were not refused.

Well, at any rate there was a saint going around from God to find out who was charitable and who was not, and he with power to reward the charitable ones. He came to the door of this poor man's house and they gave him whatever they could, like they were always accustomed when a poor person came.

'You're very good, the two of you,' says the saint to the man, 'and it isn't unknown to God that you're charitable. And I'm a saint, going around,' says he, 'and power by me from God to reward the charitable. And now,' says the saint, 'you can have three wishes, and you can ask for anything you like, and it is my advice to you to have a bit of sense for yourself and ask for something good. And I'm off back to Heaven now, and the blessings of God on you!'

And between the surprise and everything, the poor man had not a word out of him, except to lift his cap to the saint and say, 'Thank you, Sir'.

Well he never said a word to the wife, but all the time thinking and thinking what he would ask for. And he was out the next day digging the farmer's potatoes, and it was a misty kind of a day, a cold, wet mist, and by the evening his heart was broken from the cold and the wet and the misfortune. And when he came in home it was not much better, with the fire quenched on Joaney, and they without a match in the house to light it, and nothing for his supper but a pointer of mixed griddle bread without a bit of butter or a sup of sour milk.

'I declare to God, woman, but it is the hard life we have,' says he, 'without a bite or a sup to go with the bread, and I wish,' says he, 'that I had a thick black pudding up before me on the table and it as round as the griddle that bread was baked on!'

The next thing they heard was a clap of thunder, and down came the biggest black pudding they ever saw on the table and it steaming hot. Well, Joaney started to screech with the dint of fright, and he had to explain the whole story to her. And it was another kind of screeching she started then, with every name she was calling him, and every bad thing that came into her head, for being such an *amadán* as to lose the fine wish on a lump of a black pudding.

He was a patient sort of a poor man, and he would want to be and he tied to a virago like Joaney with a tongue that would raise blisters on the blacksmith's anvil. But the patience broke on him in the end, and it would be hard to blame him. 'It is too much talk you have, woman!' says he, 'and I wish to God that the same old pudding you have all the talk about would be stuck in your nose like a pig-ring, to see would it quieten you!' and the word was not out of his mouth when there it was, hanging from her nose, and all the pulling in the world would not get it off. The screeching she had before was nothing to the screeching and bawling she had now, until he was in dread that she would draw what was in the parish of people in on top of them, so that he had to use his last fine wish to take it off of her. And even that did not stop the run of speech out of her, so that in the end he left her there entirely and took off for America. And wasn't it well that the saint had his suspicions from the start that it was the foolish thing he would do with the three fine wishes?

5: The Gambler and the Hare

There was a man in this parish once and he was a dreadful gambler. He would bet on anything, but most of all he had a great wish for playing cards. He would stay up until the dawn, yes, faith, and from that until midday if anyone would hold playing with him. Well, one Shrove Tuesday night he was playing late in a farmer's house, and when midnight came the man of the house said it was time to stop, because it was the start of Lent and it was not right to play cards during Lent. The gambler began to grumble, saying he did not care what day or what time of the year it was, that he was ready to play cards with anyone any time. But all the company refused to play any more, because it was the start of Ash Wednesday. And the gambler went off on his road home, very dissatisfied.

He was not gone very far, and it a bright moonlight night, when he saw the thing moving towards him on the road, and he saw it was a hare. You know well that the hare is nervous, and that he runs for his life or else tries to go ahide when he sees you. But there wasn't a sign of dread on this hare, but to face up to the gambler as bold as you please, and stood in front of him.

'You are the man,' says the hare, 'that is ready to play cards with anyone any time. Well, here I am, and where is your deck of cards?'

The gambler was greatly in dread, but the wish for the cards was too strong for him, and he pulled out his deck and the two of them sat down on the ditch of the road and they began to play. And the gambler lost nearly every game. He lost all the money he had about him, and all he had put away. Then he put his land and his stock on the best of three games, and the hare won them one after the other. And the gambler was thinking to himself that, whatever about the money, it was not likely that a hare would come with bailiffs to put him off his land. But the hare only looked at him, and gave a laugh out of him. 'It is when you least expect me that I'll be taking your share,' says the hare. And with that, the gambler got such a fright that he fell down in a dead faint. And the people found him, and they going to Mass the next morning, and he nearly stiff with the cold.

Well, from that day on nothing went right with him. It was a cow dying here and a calf there and a sheep being killed by dogs another day, so that in the end there was not a beast of any kind living on the farm. And the crops were failing too, and the fields full of weeds and the ditches falling down into the dikes. So that in the end he had to leave the place entirely, and take to the roads. But it was noticed that if ever he was in a house where a game of cards was started, he would make some excuse to leave, and it was noticed, too, that the world and all of hares were to be seen in the neglected land, until someone else took it up and brought order on it again.

6: Carroll the Car Man

A long time ago there was a Carroll man living below in Gortnagross. He had a tidy small farm, but the principal way of living he had was carring goods across the country, the same as all his people, and the name he went by was Carroll the Car Man. One of the things he would do most of all was to carry the butter to the big butter market in Cork. He would have a big car load of it, a firkin or maybe two from every house in the townland, and when he had the butter sold he would bring back the money and give everyone the exact penny that was owing to him. And he going to Cork he would stay the first night in Newmarket and the second at a place called the Half Way, between Mallow and Cork, and be in to the market early in the day to sell. And he would leave Cork the same evening and stay that night at the Half Way again. There were a lot of car men staying at the Half Way in those times.

Well, this evening he was leaving Cork, and the butter sold, when a man he knew from the market came up to him.

'Carroll,' said he, 'I'd say you have a good few pence for the neighbours' butter. And my advice to you is to hide it well, for I hear there are robbers on the road.'

Carroll was very thankful to him, and he took the money – it was all in gold sovereigns – and put it into the little bag of oats he had with him for the horse. Well, he wasn't too far from the Half Way, when out across the ditch to him with three men and guns in their hands.

'Stand and deliver,' says they.

'How could I deliver and I having nothing?' says poor Carroll.

They searched him and the car, but they did not come on the gold, and they let him go his road. But he was very much in dread of them, that they would follow him and rob him, and the fright was so great on him that when he came as far as the Half Way he forgot the money in the oats bag, and only ran into the house where he used to stay.

They knew him well, and they put up his supper to him, and he was half way through it when he remembered the money, and out with him to the yard.

'Where is my little bag of oats?' says he.

'It is how I am after giving it to the horse,' says the yard boy. 'And by the same token, he has signs of wanting it, and the ribs out through him.'

Well, the horse had the oats eat, and the gold along with it, and Carroll had nothing to do but wait for what might happen.

He told them he'd have to spend the night out in the stable with the horse, that it was a queer kind of a horse. And all during the night he stayed awake, watching the horse's droppings and gathering up the sovereigns out of it. By the time the morning came the people of the house were dying with inquisitiveness, wanting to know what he was doing with the horse, and the man of the house went out and watched him through a hole in the door of the stable. By this time Carroll had most of the money found, all to five or six pounds, and the man of the house saw it all happening. 'That kind of a horse might be useful,' says he to himself.

After the breakfast, when they were all tackling up for the road, out with him to Carroll. 'Will you sell the horse?' says he.

'Faith and I will not,' says Carroll. 'That is a most useful horse, and I have a long road back to Athea,' says he.

'Look here,' says the man of the house, 'I'll swap the best horse I have for yours,' says he, 'and give you a hundred pounds to boot.'

'It is a bargain,' says Carroll. He knew well why the man of the house wanted to buy. And they made the bargain and swapped the horses, and away with Carroll back to his own place. And the Half Way man spent the rest of the day watching the horse, and faith at first he got a few sovereigns, but it wasn't long until the bank broke and no more was coming. And when his wife heard all about it she began scolding and barging, and she held that way day and night until he was bothered from her. And finally she would give him no peace until he followed Carroll for the money.

It was not long after that when a boy came galloping on a donkey to tell Carroll that there was a strange man asking for him through the parish. And Carroll half knew who it was, and he got ready. 'Put down a big pot of potatoes straight away,' says he to his wife, 'and a big pot of bacon and cabbage along with it, for we might have a visitor to the dinner.' It was not long until they were well boiled, and Carroll had an eye up the road. And he saw the Half Way man a long distance up the road, asking the way at a house.

'Quick,' says he to his wife. 'Give me a hold of the two pots and let you quench that fire and sweep the hearth the same as if there was never a fire there.'

And she threw out the fire and swept the hearth and put an old stool in its place with a bag of meal on top of it. And there was a big beam across the kitchen from wall to wall, with a lot of hooks on it to hang the bacon when they would have a pig killed; you know what I mean, the meat-stick. And Carroll jumped up on the table and hung the two pots off the meat-stick.

The next thing was that the man from the Half Way was in on top of them, and every swear out of him, demanding his money. And Carroll didn't make any bones about it, he had the money ready in a bag, all innocent. And he told the Half Way man to sit down with them and eat a bit, that the road was long and maybe he would be hungry. And the stranger was looking around, surprised that there was no fire and no sign of a dinner.

'Leap up there now,' says the wife, 'and hand me down the pot that boils from itself, until I see if they are done.' Up with him, and he handed down the pot, and steam rising from it. And the potatoes were grand and floury. 'Wait now, until I strain them,' says she, 'and let you strain the cabbage and cut a wedge of the bacon to that decent man.'

And the Half Way man had not a word to say, and he could hardly eat the dinner, he was so choked with curiosity.

'In the name of God,' says he, 'what sort of pots are they at all?'

'Well,' says Carroll, 'you know how it is with me, on the road carring every second day. And how would I have time to be cutting and saving turf? I'm telling you that herself here would have the sore back from gathering sticks and *brosna* for the fire if it was not for the same pots. There is great saving of firing in them, and they are very rare and wasn't it my grandfather that was lucky to get them from an old wise woman behind in Kerry?'

Well, to make a long story short, nothing would do the Half Way man but to get one of the pots, and he would not take a penny of the money for the horse, only the pot. And away home with him.

Well, if the wife was cross about the horse, it was nothing

to the tear she was in about the pot. She was fit to be tied, calling him all the names she could think of, and she screeching at the top of her voice so that she was heard at the other end of the parish. And nothing would do her but he would make off again for Gortnagross to give back the pot and get his money, for she knew well that he was kind of soft, and there was no such thing as a pot that could boil from itself.

Well, Carroll the Car Man knew well that he would be on again looking for his money, and he twice as vexed as before, on account of the pot. So Carroll says to his wife: 'Let you kill a goose, and have it ready for the dinner when he comes, to know would it soften him a bit.' And when the wife was killing the goose, Carroll got the old bladder of a pig that was around the house somewhere and let the blood of the goose into it. And she put down the goose to roast, and her husband told her to put the bladder of blood inside her bodice and to pretend nothing about it, but to play up to him when the Half Way man arrived.

Well, he came, and after a lot of persuasion they made him sit down with them to the goose, and he ate a fine dinner in spite of everything. And when the dinner was finished, Carroll said that he would have to take a sup for the road.

'Go up in the room, woman, and bring down the bottle of whiskey,' says he.

'What whiskey are you talking about?' says she.

'The whiskey that I always have about in the room,' says he, 'or is it how you are telling me that you have it drank on me?'

'And if it is, in self,' says she, playing up to him, 'isn't it well I have it earned, slaving here and tending you night and day, and you with the life of a gentleman through the country?'

'Hold your tongue, woman!' says he, giving a yell out of him, 'and get that whiskey for us, or you'll earn it!'

She made no move and with that he whipped up the carving knife and stuck her in the breast, and out with all the blood out of the bladder.

'Merciful hour! you have her killed!' says the Half Way man, and away out with him running through the country, afraid that he would be taken up for murder. And that was the last they ever heard of him.

7: The Servant Boy and the Farmer

Long ago, and it is not so long ago either, the sons and daughters of some of the smaller farmers and the labourers around here used to go down the County Limerick working as servant boys and servant girls, and the ones that had the luck to fall in with a good master and mistress were all right, but you would pity some of the poor creatures that had to put up with people that treated them badly. A lot of the big farmers down the County Limerick and over in Tipperary would grudge the bite going into your mouth and they used to try to make the hardest bargain they could with the boys and the girls that went to the hiring fairs in Newcastle and Kilmallock and the rest of the places.

Well, there was a widow-woman living in this parish long ago, and she had three sons. And this spring the oldest one of the sons said that he would go away for the year to earn a few pounds for his mother, and off he went to the hiring fair in Newcastle West. He was not long standing in the square when a farmer from the east of the county came up to him and started to make a bargain for the spring work. And it was a very queer bargain. The farmer said that he would give him twice the wages that any other farmer would offer, and he could be off home with his pay the first time they heard the cuckoo that year, but if one of them vexed the other one in any way, the bargain was finished between them, and the one that got vexed with the other would have to get twelve lashes of a whip on the back. Well, the boy was a quiet, patient fellow, and the wages seemed big to him, and he was saying to himself that it could not be so bad, and maybe it was how the farmer was making fun of him and not serious at all, and so he fixed up the bargain with the farmer, and away home to the house with them.

It was a very good spring, and the work was going very well. And the boy was a great worker, and any other farmer would be very glad to have him. But this farmer was watching him all the time and thinking how he could cheat him out of the few pounds wages, and bad and all as he was, his wife was ten times worse for all kinds of meanness and miserliness, and it would be hard to pick between the two of them for tricks and roguery. And they treated the boy well enough at first, to get as much work as they could out of him, but when the spring work was nearly getting finished, they began to persecute and torment him, trying to get him to be vexed so that he would lose the bargain, between the worst of food and calling him in the middle of the night and having him slaving away in the rain and every other dirty persecution they could think of. But patient and all as the boy was, the time came when he could stand it no longer, and he lost his temper and started to scold at the farmer and his wife. Then they had him. He had to strip down and get twelve lashes of the whip, and off home without a penny of his wages.

Well, the next spring the second brother set off for the hiring fair, and didn't he meet the same farmer, and make the very same bargain. And it was the same with him as with his brother; it was the twelve lashes of the whip he got instead of his wages after all his work.

The next spring, the third brother, the youngest one, said that he would try his luck. And the mother and the other brothers were trying to put him off going, because he was a soft sort of a lad. But he would not be said or led by them, and off with him to the fair. And it was not long before the same farmer came up to him and made the very same bargain with him, and the farmer was delighted because he thought he would have the spring work done for nothing again this year. Well, as soon as the greater part of the work was done, they began the persecution the same as before. But if they did, the boy said to himself that he might as well try a few tricks himself.

The farmer had a lot of young calves that were very much inclined to stray, and many is the time the poor boy was ordered out to find them, and warned that he would not get a bite to eat until they were all back in the paddock, and many is the hungry day he spent following them through the country. Well, this day the farmer went out early and hid the calves in the cowhouse and then he ordered the boy to look for them, and that he would not get his breakfast until he had them found.

27

'Where will I look for them, sir?' says the boy.

'You will search the likely and the unlikely, high and low, until they are found,' says the farmer.

It was not long until the farmer heard a most frightful clatter, and out with him into the haggard and he found the hay barn levelled and the boy pelting the hay and the sheaves of oats this way and that, into the muck and the water.

'What the devil are you doing, boy?' says he, letting a roar out of him.

'It is how I am searching high and low, the likely place and the unlikely,' says the boy, 'and, sure it is not how you are vexed with me?'

The farmer thought of himself. 'I am not, nor vexed. And go in and eat your breakfast,' says he.

The next day the farmer put him minding the calves again.

'You'll drive them across the river,' says he, 'and take care for fear you would get their feet wet. For if as much as one of their feet gets wet you'll be sore and sorry,' says he.

Down to the river with the boy, driving the calves. And he caught one of them and turned it upside down and dragged it across the river keeping the feet up out of the water, and when the head was down under the water the calf was drowned, and so on with all the other calves. Back with the boy to the master.

'They are across, sir,' says he, 'and I held the feet up and they are grand and dry. But maybe it was how the water was not so good for their heads,' says he.

Down with the master and there were all the calves laid out dead.

'Are you vexed with me, sir?' says the boy.

The farmer thought of himself. 'I am not, nor vexed. And you can go in to your breakfast.'

The next day was the worst day of rain that was seen for many a long year. 'We have you now,' says the farmer's wife to herself. She called the boy out of his bed. 'I'm in dread that my garden of cabbage will be robbed on me,' says she, 'and you go out now and don't leave off watching it until nightfall. And you are to keep an eye on every single head of cabbage in that garden, or it is you that will be sore and sorry,' says she.

Away out with the boy, without his breakfast, and the rain down on top of him in floods. It was not long until he was back again. And the pair inside gave under him with abuse. 'Didn't I tell you to keep an eye on the cabbage?' says the woman.

'Faith and sure, you did, ma'am,' says he, 'and isn't that what I'm after doing? I have an eye on every single head in the garden,' says he, sitting down to the table and starting to butter a big cut of bread for himself.

Out with the farmer and his wife. And the first thing they saw was every cock and hen and duck and drake and goose and gander in the place laid out dead and the eyes picked out of the head of every one of them. Over with the farmer to the paddock where he had the sheep. It was the same story, every one of them stiff, and the eyes gone out of them. Down with them to the garden, and there was an eye of one of the fowl or the sheep laid on top of every head of cabbage. The farmer was fit to be tied, but the wife calmed him.

'It is bad enough to lose the wages,' says she, 'but what about the lashes of the whip?'

'It is true for you,' says he, 'and what will we do to get rid of him before he has us beggared?'

'Wait until he goes out to the field again,' says she, 'and then I will go in hide under the hedge and make a noise like the cuckoo,' says she. And in with her in hide under the hedge.

'Come on, boy,' says the farmer, 'the day is going on us, and the ploughing is to be finished.'

'Aren't you vexed about the eyes, sir?'

'I am not, nor vexed,' says the farmer.

They started to plough the field, and it was not long until they heard every 'cuckoo, cuckoo!' out of the hedge.

'There is the cuckoo. Isn't he early this year?' says the farmer. 'And I suppose you will be making off home now?' says he.

'Faith and I will not,' says the boy. 'Go along out of that, cuckoo,' says he, 'until I finish the ploughing for this decent man!'

And with that he rises a big lump of a stone out of the ground and lets it fly at the place where the cuckoo was sounding. I tell you the song stopped in a hurry. Over with the farmer,

29

and there was the old woman, stretched out stiff on the ground, nearly dead. The farmer let out a screech and the neighbours came and lifted her into the house and sent for the priest and the doctor.

'It isn't how you are vexed with me, sir?' says the boy.

'Vexed, is it?' says he. 'And why wouldn't I be vexed with you, you devil, and you having me nearly beggared and my wife nearly killed. I'm more vexed than I ever was in my life before.'

That was it, the bargain was broken. And the farmer had to pay him out his wages and then strip down. And I tell you the boy knocked satisfaction out of him for himself and for his two brothers.

8: The Wise Men of Muing an Chait

Once upon a time there were four brothers living in a place called Muing an Chait. Their parents were dead, and there were only the four of them in the house, but they had a big farm and a lot of men working for them. But they were not very bright; indeed it would be hard to tell which of them was the biggest *amadán*, for they were constantly doing one foolish thing after another.,

Every once in a while one of them would go to the market in Newcastle with a firkin of butter for the market, and one day it fell to the lot of Tadhg, the eldest brother to take the butter, and so he set off bright and early, on a saddle horse with the firkin tied to the saddle behind him. Of course he could not take it easy, but galloping the horse as fast as he could because he thought he would be late for the market, and just at the top of Beárna the firkin slipped and away with it rolling down the slope. 'You are making speed all right,' says Tadhg, 'but if you are I'll be at the bottom of the hill before you!' Away with him, galloping as fast as the horse could go, but instead of jumping the fence where the butter fell, what he did was to continue along the road down to the foot of the hill. Of course there was no sign of the butter to be seen there; it was stuck in a bush or a dike somewhere up the slope. Well, he waited for an hour or more, to see would the firkin come, but, of course, if he was waiting until now, the firkin would not arrive where he was. Away home with him and his heart in his boots.

There was no great welcome for him at home, after losing the butter, and the three brothers were at him until, finally, he spoke up for himself. 'Well, then, and if you are so smart, what would you do in my place?' says he.

They all began to tell what they would do. Diarmaid, the next oldest said that the right thing to do was to go down to the market and buy another firkin of butter, and then to let it fall down where the first one went, and it would follow the same course, and the two firkins would come together, so that all that was to be done was to watch the second firkin carefully to find the first. But that would not do at all for Seán, the next in age, and he said that the right thing to do was to go on down to the market and call in to the police barracks, for surely some honest person would have the butter, and would leave word with the police or someone else in the town.

'Nonsense!' says Séamas, the youngest brother. 'The right thing to do is to get the bellman to go around the market, ringing the bell and announcing that whoever had the butter would get a half of it as a reward when he gave it back to the right owner.'

Shortly after that, when the next firkin was made, my bold Tadhg started out for the market again, and it was not long until he was back with the same story. The firkin was after falling off the saddle in the same place at the top of Beárna Hill. Away with the three other brothers, each of them going to put his own plan to work. Diarmaid bought the second firkin and let it off with the hill, and, if he did, he could not find either the first or the second, for the place was full of bushes and holes, although he spent until nightfall poking around looking for it. Seán headed for the barracks, but it seems that no honest person turned up with the missing firkin. Séamas paid the bellman to go around announcing the whole story, how the butter was lost and how the other two had failed to find it, and how a reward would be given to the one who gave it back to the right owner. But the upshot of that was that all the crowd at the market were splitting their sides laughing at the wisdom of the men from Muing an Chait.

They had a great discussion at home that night. They talked about it until all hours of the morning, and in the end they fixed that butter-making was no way of making money, and that they would start growing turnips instead. But they were very cautious, for turnips were not very common at the time, and they knew very little about them. So they only put down one drill of them the first year. Well, the turnips grew, and when they were nice and big, they sent Tadhg to the market, but they gave him only one turnip so that they could see what kind of sale it would make. Off with him on his saddle-horse, and the turnip tied with a bit of a cord to the saddle behind him. And of course, as you might expect, it was just at the top of Beárna Hill that the cord gave way, and off with the turnip rolling down the hill, and my brave Tadhg after it. He was not going to let it get away from him, like the butter.

Well, about half way down the first field there was a great big clump of furze bushes, and it was into the middle of that the turnip went, and what was it but that there was a big hare having a rest inside in the clump, and, of course, when the turnip came tearing and clattering in through the furze bushes, the hare did not wait for any more, but put from him as fast as his legs would carry him along the side of the hill. That knocked a start out of poor Tadhg. He stopped staring after the hare, with his eyes and his mouth open. 'Well, could you beat that?' says he. Away home with him, as fast as the horse could gallop, and in to the brothers with the story. 'Oh lads, our fortune is made!' says he, 'for it isn't turnips we have at all, but horses' eggs! Didn't the one I had fall from me, and what came out of it but the grandest little foal, and he running like the wind out across the mountain!'

They started to blame him for losing the foal, but he told them to hold their tongues, for hadn't they forty or fifty more turnips abroad in the haggard? And all they had to do, says he, was to hatch them out, and wouldn't they be the sight into the

32

fair of Newcastle with their herd of forty or fifty horses. No
sooner said than done. They brought all the turnips in and
spread them out on the floor of the stable, and gave a good part
of the evening trying to make an old mare they had to lie down
on them, to hatch them out. But, when they came out in the
morning the mare had every single turnip trampled into the
muck and bedding on the floor of the stable.

They had a long discussion about what was to be done
next, for it was clear to them that there was no profit in growing the turnips. And, of course, as usual, they spread the story
around the parish, and what was in it was laughing at them
and their horses' eggs. But finally one of the neighbours persuaded them that the right thing to do was for one of them to
get married, in the hope that the wife might talk a bit of sense
into him. They said it was a good idea, and they had great discussion about who was to take this dreadful step for the good
of the whole family, and finally they decided that Tadhg was
the one to get married, although he put against it as much as he
could. But they wouldn't listen to him, and in the heel of the
hunt, they made a match for him with the daughter of a strong
farmer from the County Kerry.

The day of the wedding came, and Tadhg was very low in
courage. He called the brothers to one side, and says he to
them: 'Lads, do you remember when we were small and our
mother was alive? She used to give us a wallop of the stick
whenever we did anything she didn't like. And what am I to do
at all, if this one starts the same game? And she is not a tidy little woman like our mother was, but a great big strong girl. If
she starts on me, mightn't she kill me before she is finished with
me? What am I to do at all when I am at her mercy?'

It was a hard question, and the marriage was delayed for
the best part of an hour while they were fixing it. It was Séamas
that thought of the plan.

'If she starts to kill him,' says he, 'it will surely take her a
while to finish him off entirely. And he will be able to put one
roar out of him at the very least. And the servant boy will hear
him in the yard, and he will put a roar out of him. And then the
man threshing in the barn will hear that and he will let out a

33

frightful screech out of him. And we will be deaf entirely if we don't hear either the one or the other of them, and we will run in and save him. Don't be in dread, now, but depend on your brothers to protect you,' says he to Tadhg, 'and moreover,' says he, 'we will make a strict rule that no stick or weapon thicker than your little finger is to be left inside the door of the house. Although, indeed, that will do you little good, and the house full of every kind of weapons, between sweeping brushes, and hatchets and tongses, and mashers and fleshforks and bittles. Sure, even the handle of the barrel-churn itself is there under her hand, ready to split you at any minute!' They all agreed that the whole thing of getting married was very dangerous, and they all promised Tadhg every kind of help if it came to the worst.

Strange to say, nothing of the kind happened, but great peace in the house, and as time went on they all said that it was the lucky day that the neighbour had hit on the plan of one of them getting married. After a while the married pair had a young son, and they called him Taidhgín, for he was the image of his father. Indeed, he was very like the father in more ways than one, for he wasn't very bright, and that was a great surprise to them all, for the mother was a very capable woman. She did her best to brighten Tadhg, but she might as well be idle, for the foolishness was hardened in him. She was doing some good with Taidhgín, whatever, but she had to be watching him and correcting him all the time, because, like the father, he had no desire for his books or for any little job around the house.

Well, one day she was after giving him a great scolding, and he was very down in the mouth. Out to the barn with him, where his father was sitting down on a rock of bogdeal, smoking the pipe. 'Ulagón Ó,' says Taidhgín to the father. 'I'm scalded from that one. She's always at me, barging and scolding. And tell me this now, what misfortune was on you at all to go looking for the likes of her behind in Kerry? Isn't it we would have the great time here, myself and yourself and my uncles, if you never brought that one near the place at all? Ochón Ó! It is sorry I am that the notion of getting married ever crossed your mind.'

'It is true for you, son,' says Tadhg, 'and it is often I am thinking the same. But it is hard to be clever all the time, and it is by experience that we learn the right thing.'

It is from that story that the saying *'Tuigeann Tadhg Taidhgín'* comes, meaning that the same kind of people understand each other.

Stories from Mrs Kate Ahern

9: The Pious Man

There was a man there long ago, and he had a great name of being very holy. He was the first up the chapel on Sunday, and there was never a pattern or a mission that he wasn't at, praying all around him. And he was being held up as a good example to the sinners as a very holy man that never missed his duty. Well, he said to himself that it would be a good thing for him to count all the times he was at Mass, so he got a big timber box and he made a hole in the cover of it, and he locked the box so that no one could interfere with it in any way, and he hid the key where no one could possibly find it. And every time he went to Mass he picked up a small pebble of a stone on his way home and dropped it in through the hole in the cover of the box. And he was not satisfied with going to Mass on Sunday, and he started to go every single week day as well, and he'd be at second Mass as well as at first Mass on the Sunday, and all the time he was putting the stone into the box every time he came home from Mass.

Well, the years were going on and, like all the rest of us, he was getting old, and he was saying to himself that there must be a great heap of stones inside in the box, and that maybe he would have to get a new box, that the old one must be nearly full. He called in the servant boy. 'Pull out that box for me, boy, until I open it. And mind yourself, because it must be very heavy.'

The boy handled it. 'It is not a bit heavy, sir, but as light as you like,' says the boy. He opened it and there were only five stones inside in it. He couldn't understand it, and off with him to the parish priest with his complaint – after all his Masses was he only going to get credit for five of them, or was it how someone was bad enough to steal the stones out of his box, but how could they do that, and it locked and the key hidden, and no sign that it was ever meddled with?

Well, this parish priest had great wisdom. 'It is like this, my good man,' says he. 'It was not about the Mass you were thinking, and it was not for your neighbours that you were praying all the times that you were at Mass, but all the time thinking how pious you were and how everyone should have great respect for you. And that is a sign to you from Heaven that you heard only five of the Masses properly, and that is the only five you will get credit for. And remember that, now, the next time you go to the church.' I tell you that it is not the one that is first to the chapel that is the highest in the sight of God.

10: The Light of Heaven

There was a poor woman going the road one time, and she had two children along with her and no sign of a husband. And the only way of living she had was the charity of the people. And, faith and sure, it was very seldom that the poor would be refused a bite or a sup or a place to sleep at any farmer's door, or at the labourer's cottage, either. When a poor person asked for alms in the name of God, I tell you it would be a hardhearted person that would refuse it.

But there was a certain parish priest and he was a very strict and hard man. And he thought that this woman was leading a bad life, and he spoke against her, telling his parishioners not to have anything to do with her. And the curate of the parish tried to put in a good word for the poor woman, but the old man wouldn't listen to him. And it came about that the poor woman and her children were passing through that parish on a Christmas Eve, and the weather was perishing cold and showers of snow flying with the wind. And she couldn't put up with it, and she knocked at a farmer's door. And the woman of the house began to cry; she had pity for the poor woman, but what about the parish priest – hadn't he put a ban on her? But her husband, a big rough kind of a man, stood up and let a big swear out of him.

'By this and by that,' says he, 'parish priest or no parish

priest, it will never be said that a poor woman and her children were turned from my door on the very night that that other poor Woman was refused a lodging in Bethlehem. Let you come in, poor woman,' says he, 'and sit to the fire and eat a bite, yourself and them creatures, and I'll go and shake down a bed for you in the loft of the stable where you'll have plenty hay to keep you warm'

They all went to sleep and out in the night the woman of the house called her husband. 'Get up quick,' says she, 'for the stable is on fire. And I don't know if it was the right thing we did to let her in at all.' Out he ran, and the stable was one blaze of light. And he ran into it to save the horse, but there was no fire, only the poor woman and her two children lying dead on the hay, and a great light shining out of them. Off with the farmer to the priest's house and brought the parish priest and the curate back with him to see the wonder. And they all went into the stable, the farmer and his wife, the servant boy and the servant girl and the two priests. And faith if they did, the minute they were inside the door the great light quenched and the place was pitch dark. They felt their way out into the yard, and the minute they were outside the light came on again.

'It must be one of us,' says the curate, 'that is making the light quench, for it is a heavenly light, and one of us must be a sinner.' And he sent them in one by one, the farmer and his wife and the two servants, and they all knelt down and said a prayer for the dead, and the light stayed shining. And the curate went in, and the light stayed shining. But the minute the old priest put his leg over the threshold the light quenched.

'It is I am the sinner,' says he, 'and my sin was that I was too hard on this poor woman.'

And the very next Sunday he preached a sermon and told the congregation that he was at fault, and that no matter how bad appearances were that they should always be charitable to the poor, and let God make the judgement.

11: The Blood of Adam

There was a priest in this parish long ago, and the old people used to tell us a lot of stories about him. He was a fine singer, they said, and he could play the fiddle finely and he was very fond of music. He was a noted horseman, too, although it was a horse that killed him in the end – it was how he was out one night on a sick call, and it was late and very dark when he was coming home, and the horse stumbled and threw him, and they found him in the morning and his neck broken. It was behind on the Gort a' Ghleanna road it happened, just at the bridge half ways down the hill. Well, what I'm telling you happened a good while before that, on another night when he was out riding late, when he was back on the lower road, near the county bounds.

It was a bright moonlight night and he was walking the horse along when he heard this sweet music coming from the bank of the river, and he stopped to listen to it. After a while he put the horse at the ditch of the road and cleared it into the field and down to the river. And there was this very big crowd of small people, men and women about as big as a twelve years old child, and they all gathered around listening to a lot of them that were playing every kind of musical instrument. And the priest was sitting on his horse, enjoying the music, when some of them saw him. ''Tis a priest,' they said and the music stopped. And they all gathered around the horse.

And one of them, the head man of them, maybe, spoke up. 'Such a question, Father, and will you answer it?' says he.

'I will, and welcome, if I have the answer,' says the priest.

'What we want to know is this, will we go to Heaven?' says the little man.

'I do not know,' says the priest, 'but I can tell you this much: if you have any drop of Adam's blood in your veins, you have as good a chance of Heaven as any man, but if you have not, then you have no right to Heaven.'

'Ochon Ó!' says the little man. And they all went off along the river bank, all crying and wailing so that it would break your heart to listen to them.

12: The Coat on the Sunbeam

There was a poor man one time working for a farmer up on the mountain, and the work he had was minding the cattle, the dry stock that were left out all the year far away from the house. And it was so far away that he was able to go to Mass but seldom, but all the same he was very holy and constantly saying his prayers. And every Sunday when Mass was being said he used to go on his knees with his face turned towards the direction of the chapel where the Mass was being said and go through his prayers in a very holy way.

Well, one Sunday in the spring time he got this chance to go to Mass – I suppose it was how someone else was up on the mountain that day and offered to mind the cattle for him. It was cold enough above when he was starting out and he put his old coat around him, but when he was down off the mountain a piece the sun was getting hot and he took off the coat and carried it. And he had it across his arm during the Mass, and when it was coming in his way he laid it from him, and where did he lay it but across a sunbeam that was shining in the window, and the sunbeam kept the coat up. And when the priest turned round to speak to the people he saw the coat on the sunbeam, and he said to himself that it was a miracle and that the owner of the coat must be a very holy man. And after Mass was finished the priest talked to the poor man and advised him to go to Mass every Sunday, and that he would talk to the master and would tell him to send one of the servant boys up every Sunday so that the poor old holy man could go to the chapel. And he went every Sunday from that on. And he used to be listening to the people going to Mass, and it was not always the good word they had, some of them criticising the neighbours and spreading gossip. And one day he was listening to two women walking in front of him and cutting up the character of another woman in the place, and he was agreeing with them in his mind and saying to himself, 'She must be the right *srimileáilí* and all that talk about her!'

And when he went into the chapel he laid the coat out of

his hand on the sunbeam, but if he did, the coat fell down in a heap on the ground. And the priest saw it, and after the Mass he questioned the holy man to see what was the great sin he had committed, and when he heard about the back-biting he said that was it, that it was a worse sin than to steal from a person. And he gave him absolution and told him never to listen to that kind of talk again.

13: The Drink of Gold

There was a widow-woman one time and her son got married to a nice girl, but the old woman never made any way friendly with the daughter-in-law, and the poor girl was scalded from her, and the old woman taking care not to pretend anything to the son, for fear he would take his wife's part, and the young woman saying nothing for fear she would rise a row between mother and son. Faith, I tell you she had no easy time.

Finally the old woman took some sickness and it was plain that she was not long for this world. And she had a lot of money put aside, all in sovereigns in a bag under her mattress. And what did she decide on doing but to take it to the next world with her, or into the grave with her anyhow, for fear the daughter-in-law would get it. And there was a woman that was a long time a servant girl in the house, minding the old woman. And the old woman told her to get the bag of gold and to put it down in a skillet over the fire and to melt it, so that she could drink it and take it with her. And the servant did not know what to do. Well, the priest came to give the old woman the last sacraments, and the servant girl asked his advice.

'I don't think it is right,' says she, 'for the dying to rob the living. And, anyhow, wouldn't it burn the inside out of her if she drank it? What will I do at all, Father?'

'What you'll do, my good woman,' says he, 'is to put down a couple of pounds of butter and melt it, and give it to her. It will do her no harm, and it will satisfy her. She is wandering a bit in the head, the poor thing. And you'll give the money to the young man and his wife as soon as the old woman is gone.'

And that is what she did. She had to keep reheating the butter for two or three days, and the old woman trying to swallow it down and it putting *masmas* on her, and she certain that it was the gold. And she died happy, thinking that she had the gold taken from the daughter-in-law. There is no knowing what some people will do, with the dint of meanness and miserliness.

14: The Pig-Headed Child

Long ago, in the bad times, there were hundreds of poor people travelling the roads. Some of them were able to do a day's work or take a job with a farmer, but there were more that weren't able to work, and all they could do was to stretch out their hand for charity at the door. And the one you would pity most of all was the poor woman, a widow maybe, with young children. And it is many a one of that class of a poor person that would be dead long ago, only for the help they got from the houses along the road. And, by the same token, it is often they would get a better welcome at a small farmer's house or at a labourer's cottage than at the big house of rich people.

Well, I often heard a story about one of these poor people, the kind of a story that would frighten you. It seems that there was this poor widow going the road with a lot of children. The youngest one only an infant up in her arms and two more very small ones hanging on to her skirt and two or three more a bit bigger running around her. And the only way she could get the bite and the sup to keep them alive was to stretch out her hand at the door of the houses along the road.

There was a big house in that part of the country, belonging to a big farmer, a sort of a half gentleman. And he would be a decent generous sort of a man only for his wife. She was a devil with a miserly mind and a hungry heart that would not let her stretch out a crust of bread to a poor person and he starving. And the poor people going the road knew very well that it was no use in the world for them to go next or near her door, and, faith and sure, it was far away from her they kept. But one cold winter's day, in the evening with the darkness coming down this poor widow-woman and her children were passing the big house on the road. And the poor creature did not know what kind of a house it was, and in with her and the children up the avenue to the door, and they thinking that maybe they would get the night's lodging, to be in out of the cold, as well as a bite for their supper.

The woman of the house was sitting on a big armchair up at the front window, watching out for fear any one of the servants would be a minute idle or for fear a ha'porth of anything would go astray, and she saw the poor woman and the flock of children coming. She called down to the servant at the door. 'What do those dirty people want?' says she.

'It is a poor woman and her children that want some little help, ma'am,' says the servant.

'Tell that sow and her litter that if they are not off my land as quick as they can foot it, it is how I'll set the dogs on them!'

And the servant girl couldn't say a word with the fright, but the poor woman heard it well enough. She said nothing, but turned away with the children, God help them, the poor creatures.

But it was always said that you should never liken a Christian to a beast, and signs be on it, it wasn't long until the woman of the house had cause to regret what she said. There was a child expected in the house, and when the child was born, God bless the mark! wasn't it a little girl with a pig's head. And she grew up in the house, and until the day she died they never let her out in dread she would be seen. And she could never talk, only to squeal and grunt like a pig. And she couldn't eat or drink like a Christian either; all she could do was to eat like a pig out of a silver trough they made for her.

15: The Proud Girl

A thing that you would often see long ago, and sometimes even still is a girl or a woman walking along with a bucket of water on her head. When I was small every woman in the parish could do it. They used to have a bit of an old stocking and a nice twist of hay inside in it and it turned around for all the world like a black pudding, and they would put that on top of their head to balance the bucket and to save their head. What they had before the zinc buckets and the enamel ones were timber buckets and cans. The can had straight sides and one stave rising up above the others.

I heard a story about a girl who was going to the market one day and she had a fine can of cream on her head. And she walking along the road she was making up in her head what she would do with the money she got for the cream. She was going to buy a setting of eggs and put them to hatch, and then she would have twelve chickens when they came out. And the next year she would have twelve clutches of eggs down, and the year after that there is no knowing to the number of fowl she would have. And she was going to have the world and all of eggs for sale, and plenty of chickens at every fair and market, and she making money hand over fist. And with that big fortune, there would be no bother to her to marry a rich farmer, with the grass of forty cows, maybe. And she would have the finest dresses and coats, and a hat on her head going to Mass on Sunday. 'And,' says she to herself, 'there's them that I won't look at, nor on the side of the road they are on, but only to toss my head like this and I passing them out.' And with that she tossed her head, and down with the can of cream on the road. I always heard it said that pride goes before a fall, and isn't that the proof of it?

Stories from Dick Denihan

16: Daniel O'Connell and the Cow

It was always said that there was no fear of you in the court of law if you could get Daniel O'Connell to defend you. There was a story about a man that was brought up for stealing a cow, and at that time you could be hanged for stealing, or if you weren't hanged you'd be transported for the rest of your natural life. And the man that was bringing the case against the poor man was Counsellor Goold, the same man who was the landlord of this parish. And he was good friends with Daniel O'Connell, but they were always trying to get the better of each other in the court.

Well, the case came up, and Goold led off, accusing the poor man of the theft of the cow.

'What age was the cow?' says O'Connell.

'It was a three year old,' says Goold.

'How would you know the like of that?' says O'Connell. 'Aren't you just after buying a big estate of land off the Earl of Devon, and isn't it land so bad that if you put a three year old beast on it, the poor creature would come out of it after a year only the size of a yearling, but with horns on her like a deer from the hills of Kerry! 'Tis all nonsense, my lord,' says he to the judge. 'My friend, Mr Goold is a good and honest man, but he knows nothing about cattle. The case should be dismissed!' And Goold got so flustered with all the fun and laughing in the court that he got all mixed up, and the judge dismissed the case.

They were going out of the court, and the poor man came up to O'Connell. And Goold was there, too, talking to O'Connell. And the poor man was full of thanks and praise for the man that saved him, and all excuses that he was so poor that he had nothing to offer O'Connell for getting him off free.

'Of course you are innocent, you haven't even the cow?' says O'Connell.

He swore by this and by that that he hadn't the cow and

that he didn't know anything about it.

'Well,' says O'Connell, 'I'll forgive you the costs of the case this time, for I can well understand how poor and how honest you are. But tell me this, now, especially when my good friend Mr Goold here knows so little about cattle. Suppose that myself or my friend Mr Goold wanted to steal a good cow, and we saw a big herd of them in a field on a winter's night like last night. How would we know the best one?'

'Easy enough, sir,' says the man, 'all you have to do is to pick out the one that is the farthest out in the field from the hedge. Because that is the one that is the fattest and with the best condition. There's no bother to it at all, then, only to drive her away, but of course you'll have to have the arrangements made to sell her to a butcher before the daylight,' says he. He was so delighted at the Counsellors talking to him that he gave himself away completely.

But O'Connell and Goold only laughed. 'There now, Thomas, my friend,' says O'Connell, 'is a man that could teach us both about cattle.'

'Every man to his trade,' says Goold.

17: The Magic Fiddle

There was an old belief that if you found a brier rooted at both ends you could use it to work a spell to obtain magic powers, such as being able to 'read the cards', that means to be able to tell the face value of the playing cards held by the other man in a card game by looking at the backs of them. The person who wanted to gain power of this kind had to go to the place where the double rooted brier grew, on the morning of May Day or November Day, just as the day was dawning, and then strip naked and crawl under the brier and at the same time call on the Devil to give the power to him.

The story goes that there was a man named the Rake Ó Néill in these parts who had a great desire for music, but he could not learn a single note, although he tried to learn all sorts of instruments. Finally the desire grew so great that he went through the double rooted brier on a November Morning calling on the Devil for the gift of music. When he turned around to put on his clothes he found a queer looking fiddle with one string lying on top of the clothes, and he could not even wait to dress himself before he tried it. When he drew the bow on the string, out came the sweetest music he ever heard. The Rake was delighted – he had his wish at last. From then onwards he turned up at every dance and pattern, fair and gathering, and everyone was delighted with the music. The fiddle would play only one tune, but everyone present would prefer to listen to that tune all day and all night than to the finest musical selection that could be thought of.

One day he was playing at a fair, and a foreign gentleman who was buying horses for the King of France heard him playing and he was so taken with the music that he invited him to come and play for the King of France. The Rake had nothing against that and he set out for France with the gentleman. And for twenty years he played the same tune every night at the court of the king. And nobody grew tired of the tune; in fact they were more eager to hear it as time went on. And it was noted that no other person could play the one-stringed fiddle or even learn the tune, even though all the great musicians of France tried their best to do it.

One night when the whole of the French court was fast asleep, except for the guards at the gates, they were all woken up by a twang of music as loud as a clap of thunder. It left their heads singing for a few minutes, but when they came to themselves and searched the palace to see what was the cause of it, they found the Rake Ó Néill dead in his bed, and the fiddle, which he always had hanging over his bed at night, broken into fragments on the floor.

18: Seán na Scuab

One time long ago, below in Limerick city, they were trying to elect the mayor, and it was growing hard with them because no two of them would agree on who was to be mayor of the city. And they were like that for a long time. Whenever one of the big men of the town would say that such a one should be picked, three or four would rise up and say that he wouldn't do. And when they had no mayor to direct them, things were going very badly, trade going down and fighting in the street and no law and order at all. Well, in the latter end, one important man stood up. 'Enough of this for a story,' says he. 'There is no profit going on like this, with no sign of an agreement and things going from bad to worse every day. And what we should do,' says he, 'is to go out to Thomond Bridge, outside the castle, and the first man that crosses in from the Clare side, to make him the mayor.'

Well, when they could think of nothing better, that is what they settled on doing, and away with all the big people of the city out to the bridge, ready to take up the first man that came.

Well, there was a poor fellow living away out on the Clare side, in the middle of the bogs, and the way of living he had to support himself and his poor old mother was to be cutting the heather and making brooms and peck scrapers of it and selling them to the people all around. He was an honest sort of a poor fellow, but a bit of a half fool, a bit simple. Well one day came and he travelled a good bit with his little ass and car loaded with the brooms, and he wasn't making much sale. So in the latter end, out in the day, he came to the top of a hill where he could see the city of Limerick away a good piece from him. 'Do you know what,' says he to the ass, 'I'd say that there is a power of people living in that place, and maybe we could make good sale there.' No sooner said than done, away with him making for the city.

Well, all the big people waiting at the bridge were getting very uneasy with no one coming. So when they saw this man coming, sitting up in the car on top of his load, they all began to brighten up.

'What is your name, my good man?' says the most important man there.

''Tis Seán, sir, and 'tis Seán na Scuab they do be calling me
at home, for that is the way I have of living, always making the
heather brooms and trying to sell them.'

'Well, come on with us now, Seán na Scuab,' says the spokes-
man, 'for you are to be the mayor of this city for a year and a
day.'

Away with them to the mayor's palace, and poor Seán in
the middle of them, and he knowing as much about a mayor as
a cow about a holiday. They took off his old *giobals* of clothes,
and washed and shaved him, and dressed him in the finest
robes and put him sitting down on the mayor's high chair, and
all of them bowing and scraping in front of him and asking him
what was to be done with this and that. And, mind you, when
all is said and done he wasn't giving them bad advice at all, for
he was a very honest poor fellow, and he was very handy at
making up money in his head from selling the brooms. Of
course he had no education, he couldn't read A on the side of a
flour bag.

Well, Seán's poor old mother was waiting for him at home,
and when he wasn't coming by nightfall she began to be greatly in dread that something was after happening to him. So the
next morning she went off looking for him, asking along the
road, until she traced him into Limerick city. She asked a soldier
at the castle did he see her son, Seán na Scuab, and the soldier
started bowing to her and brought her along to the mayor's
palace, and there was great coming and going there, with mes-
sengers running in and out and important people in fine clothes
and a big guard of soldiers with spears and swords. And the
poor woman was very frightened and shy, but when they heard
who she was, Seán na Scuab's mother, they brought her in to
the finest room of all, and up to the high chair where this
important looking man was sitting giving all sorts of orders out
of him.

'Is it how you don't know your own son, mother?' says he.

'Well, glory be to God, Seán *a mhaoineach*,' says she. 'Sure

49

I'd never know you at all, and you dressed like that!'

'Faith and sure, mother,' says Seán, 'it would be hard to blame you when I hardly know myself!'

Well, they dressed the poor old woman out in fine clothes, and she the mayor's mother, and she never saw a poor day again.

19: The Fool and the Feather Mattress

Long ago it was all feather mattresses, or ticks as they used to be called, that people would have to sleep on. And it was not everyone had them, because of course it would take the feathers of more than a hundred geese to stuff a really big thick one. Of course, it was only the soft feathers of the breast of the goose or the duck or the hen that would be put into a good tick. And a good one was a lot more comfortable than the hair mattresses that's going now, and there was nothing softer or warmer on a winter's night.

Well, there was this poor fellow, and he was a sort of a half-fool, harmless, you know, but without much sense or understanding. And one day he heard two women boasting about the fine feather ticks they were after making, how soft they were and all the fine feathers that went into them, and how warm and comfortable they were going to be. And the poor half-fool never had a chance to sleep on the like, for his people were only very poor, and it is only a handful of straw they would have under them at night. And he was saying to himself that he would like to try sleeping on feathers, to see what it was like. And this day he was going along the road, and what should he meet but a dead goose lying on the side of the road. Over with him and pulls a handful of feathers off the breast of the goose. It was a fine hot day, and what did he do but to spread out the feathers on the side of the road and lie down on them for a rest. He wasn't long there when he heard someone coming, a neighbouring farmer.

'What is wrong with you Johnny? Is it how you are sick or

is it a weakness you have?' says the farmer, full of compassion for the poor boy.

Up with Johnny off of the road. 'Faith, upon my soul, it is not,' says he, 'but I'm telling you that I wouldn't long be getting stiff lying on the feathers. And if it is so hard to lie down on a small handful of them, it must be a right martyrdom entirely to have to spend the night lying on top of a big bag full of them. Ochón Ó, it is out of their minds they are, to be sleeping on anything as hard as feathers, and loads of straw in the country!'

20: The Fairy Path

It is well known that you should never interfere with a fairy path. The old people always said that there were paths through the country and that the fairies used to be travelling along them from place to place, and that if you dug up the path or put any kind of an obstruction on it, you would not be in the better of it. There is many a story about what happened to the man that interfered with one of them, and here is one that I often heard.

It seems that there was a man in the County Limerick and he was building a new house. He was a well-to-do farmer, with the grass of fifty cows, and he could well afford to build any kind of a house anywhere he liked. But nothing would do him but to build his new house down on a place that the old people said was a fairy path. And they warned him against it and still it was no good. Not one sign of notice did he take of them or their warning. And according as he was building the house, everything was going against him. The scaffolding was falling down and the mortar wouldn't mix properly for them, and when the mason hit a stone with his hammer, it split the wrong way or fell in dust. And he was losing his temper and swearing that he'd best the fairies yet. He put masons and labourers working night and day on the house, for often what they built in the day was levelled again during the night, and by working day and night he was beating them. He was losing a power of money by the house. He would have ten houses built for what it was

51

costing him. But he wouldn't give in, and finally the house was built.

He was in his new house only a couple of months, and by this time it was the dead of winter, when one night he thought he would go to a neighbour's house for a game of cards. It was as quiet a night as you ever saw, but it was as black as pitch, so he twisted a handful of straw into a *sopóg* and lit it in the fire to give him a light out through the yard, for fear he'd hit against a tankard or a plough or anything. And he was just at the yard gate when this mighty blast of a *sidhe gaoithe* nearly knocked him down. And it took the *sopóg* out of his hand, and it all in a flame and threw it up on the roof of the house, and with the dint of the wind the whole of the thatch was one blaze of fire before two minutes, and the sparks were flying in every direction, and in another couple of minutes the thatch of every shed and *cróitín* in the place was going up in fire. The neighbours came running with buckets, but the pump in the yard that never before was known to fail was as dry as dust that night and before they could get water the whole place was burned down, and not one thing could be saved except his wife, and she terrified, the poor woman, and the children with nothing on them but their little nightshirts. I'm telling you that the next time he built a house it was far from the fairy path he built it.

21: The Soup Stone

There was a poor travelling man going the roads, and it is often he was cold and hungry. Well, one day he was saying to himself that a drink of hot soup would do him all the good in the world, and he knew a farmer's house where the woman was kind of soft, and he made up his mind to try his luck there. Down with him to the brink of the river and he picked up a nice round stone about the size of an apple, and in with him to the farmer's house, and asked the woman would she give him a pan and a small drop of clean warm water, and so she did. And he was washing and cleaning the stone until he had it shining.

'You have great washing of the stone, my poor man,' says she.

'And why not I, ma'am, and it a soup stone,' says he.

'Is it how you could make soup of it?' says she.

'It is, indeed, and the best of soup,' says he.

'Glory be to God, and could anyone do it?' says she.

'Not a sign of bother on them to do it, but to watch the one that knows how to make it,' says he.

'Why then, I'd be greatly obliged to you,' says she, 'and there is the pot and there is the fire and plenty water.'

He put down about half a gallon of water in the pot, and the stone inside in it. And the two of them were watching it.

'A shake of salt and pepper would do it no harm,' says he.

She gave him the pepper and the salt. After a while, and the water beginning to boil: 'It isn't thickening so well,' says he, 'a shake of flour would do it no harm.'

She put a good handful of white flour in the pot.

'And that bone of a leg of mutton that you're going to throw to the dogs,' says he, 'would do it no harm at all, 'but great good, maybe.'

She had no notion of throwing it to the dogs, and plenty meat on it, but she wouldn't give it to say that she was keeping it for her husband's supper, and down it went into the pot.

'There will be great strength in it now,' says he, 'but a few potatoes would do it no harm.'

It was herself that peeled half a dozen of the potatoes, and down with them. It was boiling up now, and getting fine and thick.

'Do you know what,' says he, 'I'm thinking that a couple of them fine big onions would put a finish on it.' No sooner said than done, and the soup boiled away for half an hour or so.

''Tis ready now,' says he, 'and maybe you'd like a taste of it.'

'Oh, the least drop,' says she, getting two piggins and filling out the soup into them, about a quart in each. I tell you it went down sweetly. 'That is fine soup,' says she, 'and I'm much obliged to you for showing me how to make it.'

'What did I tell you?' says he, 'but that you could make the finest of soup out of a soup stone?'

He rested himself for a while, and had a smoke of her husband's tobacco. And off he went. And the foolish woman never stopped boasting of how she could make soup out of a stone, and all the neighbours laughing behind their hand at her. But I'd say it was a long time before the travelling man came around that part of the country again.

22: The Snuff Box

You know that little grove of beech trees on the left hand side of the road halfways up the green hill between Athea bridge and Colbert's. Well, there is a gap going into it and it is there that the spirit used to stand every night. It was the ghost of a woman that was dead a few years, a poor travelling woman that was found dead one winter's morning just inside the gap. It was how she got weak going up the hill from the village and went in behind the ditch for a bit of shelter and no one saw her until she was dead. And she used to be standing at the gap every night, with her hand out and something in it and she offering it to anyone that passed the road. And the people knew well that it was a ghost and they were afraid to cross up or down at that time of the night.

Well, there was a man from Glenagore in the village one night and he had a drop taken and the boys were joking him about the ghost, and saying he would have to take the roundabout way over by the old church. 'Faith, and I will not,' says he, 'when it is fifty ghosts, maybe, I'd see and I passing the old church. I'd rather one than fifty, and I always heard that she was a poor harmless creature.' So off he went. And there was the ghost before him, and her hand out with the thing in it. And my man would not be daunted and he went over and looked at it. And it was a fine snuff box, silver, it was, with grand jewels and ornaments on it. And what did he do, out of bravado, but take a pinch of snuff.

'*Beannacht dílis Dé le h-anaman na marbh!*' says he, taking a fine pinch.

She did not say a word, but to hold out the box again, and he took another pinch and said the prayer for the dead, like we always do when we get a pinch of snuff or a pipe of tobacco. And the third time again.

And then she spoke. 'Something I did when I was alive,' says she, 'that has me here doing my purgatory until someone would pray for my soul three times. And you did it. And now you can keep the snuff box, and it will never be empty as long as you don't tell anyone where it came from.'

She was never seen there again, and my man had the snuff box and it always full no matter how much was taken out of it. And everyone was after him for a pinch of fine snuff. And that went on for a few years. But he was fond of a drop, as I said, and he had a loose mouth when he had it taken. And one night in the public house he told the story, how he got it. And from that minute on the box was empty. He couldn't keep his mouth shut, but of course if he did we would not have the story. And you should always say a prayer for the dead when you take a pinch of snuff or a pull of the pipe from anyone.

23: The Tailor and the Hare Woman

I suppose you often heard that the tailors long ago used to go around the country working with this farmer and that, making whatever clothes were wanted in the house? Well, there was a travelling tailor by the name of Hegarty, and when he came to a certain townland he always stayed with one farmer there, and he was well known in the house. Well, he was on his travels when he heard that this farmer was after dying, and the next time he was in that townland he called in to the widow, to tell her how sorry he was for her trouble. And she told him that he could stay in the house the same as always. He was working away in the house until May Morning came, and he was a very light sleeper, and some sound like splashing water woke him up early.

'Glory be to God,' says he. 'The widow is making the breakfast already,' and he jumped out of bed and put his head out the door of the loft, for it was in the loft over the lower room he had his bed, the same as always.

But when he saw what was going on in the kitchen he came no farther out but only stood there with his eyes and his mouth open. She was running out the door with a big wooden can and drawing water as fast as she could and filling a big tub that she had right in the middle of the kitchen. And every time she spilled a can of water into the tub she took the tongs and put a little bit of a red cinder from the fire into the water. When the tub was full she held awhile saying verses that he could make no sense of, and when she had enough verses said she threw down every stitch of clothes off her and jumped into the tub and splashed the water over herself. And the next minute she was changed into a big grey hare, and away out the door with her. About half an hour after, and the tailor still looking out through the door of the loft, in with her again and into the tub and changed back into her own shape, and put on her clothes. He tiptoed back to his bed, and after a while she called him to his breakfast. He didn't pretend anything, nor pass any remark, but the whole thing had him puzzled, and small blame to him.

The next morning he heard the splashing again, and she changed into the hare and away with her. And, faith, if she did the tailor wasn't far behind her, because all he did was to throw off the nightshirt and jump into the tub and sure enough he turned into a hare as well as she did. And away with him after her. Away with her up to the top of the hill, and the tailor close behind her. And there was a nice smooth patch of grass there, and about twenty hares gathered. And a great big old hare stood up and looked around him at the other hares.

'Home with you all!' says he, 'we can do no good today, for there is a stranger amongst us!' And the hares all scattered east and west.

And, faith, the tailor wasn't slow in moving either, but away with him as fast as he could, and the hare-woman out before him. And she was in the door of the house before him and into the tub and out the other side in her own shape just as he was coming in the door. And she caught the tub and flung it over on its side. But the tailor made a dive and met the water coming out of the tub, and changed back into his own shape too. And I can tell you he made no delay up the stairs and on with his clothes, and it was lucky for him that he was a small little man or he would never be able to climb out the loft window in the gable of the house and she waiting for him at the foot of the loft ladder, and a kettle of boiled water in her two hands, ready to scald him alive.

He didn't stop, between running and walking, until he put the length of the parish between him and that house. And late in the day he went into another farmer's house and started to work there the same as always. He was up on the table, working away, cutting and sewing. And out in the evening one of the children of the house climbed up on the table alongside him to see the work, and whatever look he gave at the tailor's neck – 'What is that thing stuck to the back of your neck, sir?' says the little boy.

And when the tailor put up his hand he found that the back of his neck was covered with hare's fur. It was the one place that the water did not touch when she spilled it out of the tub. I tell you he kept far away from that townland from that day on. And ever after he kept a scarf tight around the back of his neck, so that the patch of fur would not be seen.

STORIES FROM JOHN HERBERT

24: The Midnight Mass

You know the old graveyard below at Ranasaer? Well, I'll tell you a queer thing that happened there. A part of the old church is standing there yet, and the people used to say that a light would be seen in it from time to time, but they were all in dread of whatever might be in it, and no one would go near the place after dark. There was a man that was strange to the place going past one night late. He was from the Dromcolliher side and he was walking home from Rathkeale after doing some business, and it was a bright moonlight night. He knew nothing about the old church ruin and he never heard any of the stories about it, and so, when he saw the lights inside – he could see that it was a churchyard – he said to himself that maybe it was grave robbers or something bad going on, and that he should take a look at whatever it was. In with him across the field to the wall of the burying ground. It was all quiet, only the light burning inside in the ruin, and he could not see what it was, and so he went in over the wall without a sound and stole over to the window. And there were two wax candles in sconces on the altar and the priest in his vestments. The Dromcolliher man could not make out what was going on until the priest turned around and said, 'Is there anyone here who will answer my Mass?' And the man outside says to himself that it was a queer time of the night to be saying Mass, and a queer place too, but he supposed it was all right, and maybe that it was some new rule that a Mass was to be said now and again in the old places where it used to be said before the English burned our old churches.

And with that he spoke up, and told the priest that he would serve the Mass. And so he did: the priest said the Mass and he gave the answers and did everything that the server does in the chapel on a Sunday.

And when it was finished the priest turned and spoke to him. 'Now I can rest in peace,' said the priest. 'Once a year,' said he, 'for more than two hundred years I am coming back here looking for someone to answer my Mass. I was a priest in a religious order, and we were supposed to say a certain number of Masses, and I neglected to say one of them. And one day the soldiers came and killed us all. And the other priests that had their duty done were let into Heaven, but I could not get in until I had said that Mass, and a living person would have to witness it. And I am very thankful to you. And go your road now in safety,' says he, and he lifting up his hand the way a priest gives you a blessing.

And the man got up from his knees. 'Good night to you, Father, and God bless you!' says he, and away out to the road with him. And when he looked back there was not a sign of the light or the priest to be seen, only the moonlight shining on the old ruin.

25: The Prophecy

There was a king there long ago, and he was very rich and powerful, and the only thing that was troubling himself and his wife, the queen, was that they had no children. Well, at long last there was a child coming, and the king was in great fuss about it, he had priests and bishops and wise men and doctors and nurses all ready. And just before the child was born, it was in the middle of the night, he brought all the wise men up to the top of the castle, and told them to read the stars and tell him about the child's future. And there was one of the wise men that could read the stars and make prophecies from them, and he told the child's future.

'The child will be a boy,' said the wise man, 'and he will grow up strong and handsome and clever. There is no son of a king in the whole world that will be his equal,' said the wise man, reading the stars all the time. 'But what is this? Ochón, the bad story! It is written in the stars that when the son of the king is twenty-one years of age, he is to be killed by a flash of lightning.' And the wise man wrote down the message on paper and handed it to the king, that twenty-one years exactly from the day he was born, the son of the king would be hit by lightning and killed.

The child was born the same night, a fine boy. And he grew up just as the wise man prophesied; there was not a king's son in the world that was his equal in handsomeness or in learning or in strength or in courage, and the people of the kingdom would do anything for him. And the old king never told a single person about the prophecy, and he warned the wise man to say nothing about it either, or it would be the worse for him. The king was greatly frightened and troubled by the prophecy, but he did not want to be putting trouble and sorrow on his son and on the queen and on all the people, and that is why he kept it to himself.

But when the son of the king was coming to about nineteen years old he noticed his father directing a great big crowd of masons and workmen putting up a great big fortification of some sort on the side of a hill about a mile away from the king's castle, and the old king would not let him into the fortification or even tell him what it was or what it was for. The masons knew but as little, but they only knew they were to build a wall here and a door there and a window somewhere else according as the king directed them, until the building was all finished. And the day before his twenty-first birthday, the king took his son to one side and showed him the paper and told him about the prophecy.

'And now,' said the king, 'I am going to put you into the big fortification, and you are to stay there until all the thunder and lightning is over. And you can be sure that no lightning will touch you there, and the height of stone and mortar that I have put over it.'

So the king's son went into the fortification and sat down. And there was plenty to eat and drink there, but he had no mind for eating and drinking. He was greatly troubled by what the king told him. And he was thinking to himself that if it was the will of God that he would be killed, all the stone and mortar in Ireland would not save him. And finally he got so troubled that he could not stand being inside in the fortification any more, so he searched around until he found an open window, for the old king had the doors locked and barred. He crept out through the window, and away down to the river and threw himself down on the mossy bank. It was a fine hot day in the beginning of August, and it was not long until he fell asleep.

And while he was asleep the dark clouds came across the sky, and the thunder and lightning began. And there came a most frightful flash of lightning and a band of thunder, and the lightning hit the fortification and made dust of it. And the king and all the people came running out in the rain, and every *ulagón* out of them, in dread the king's son was killed. But the next thing was that they saw him coming up from the river, and all the danger past, and the mourning was not long turning to rejoicing. And when the old king died, his son was the king of that kingdom for many years.

26: The Headless Coach

Did you ever hear about the headless coach? Well, I did more than hear about it, for I was as near to it as I am to you now. I was only a *garsún* at the time, and one night in the winter time my mother told me to go out to the rick of turf and to bring in a bag of dry turf to keep the fire going, on account of the cold that was there. Well, it was a bright moonlight night, and I was not one sign afraid, and off with me and my bag on my shoulder, and, sure, it was only about fifty yards to the rick, where the turf was at the side of the road; it was not really a rick but a heap, for it was only just after being brought from the bog. Well, I had it full when I heard the noise of wheels. And there was more noise than you'd have from a trap or a common car, and I thought it must be a threshing machine, for this was early in the winter, and the threshing machines were still on the go. And it was coming nearer by the sound of it, and I shoved in against the hedge, because the road was narrow, and I was afraid that it might hit against me. And, may the Lord save us! the noise came apast me on the road. And I could feel a bit of a shake in

61

the road the same as you would any time a heavy load was passing you out. And I could not make out what it was. I was not a bit in dread then, I thought all the time it must be a threshing machine or some other heavy load. And I bent down on my knee to see it against the moonlight. And the noise and the shaking went apast me, and there was not a sign of anything to be seen. And you wouldn't see me running home with the speed I made. If there was a hare or a hound out in front I'd have him passed before he was half way to the house. And they refused to believe me at home, but I wouldn't go back for the bag, and my father had to go for it.

A couple of days after that I was talking to an old man that lived near us, and I told him about the noise.

'*Go bhfóiridh Dia orainn!*' says he, 'but it was the Headless Coach. And any time it comes, it is sure to leave some *mácail* behind it.'

And there was a young lad going the road a few weeks after that. And he was passing our turf, at the very place I heard the noise, and didn't he get a stumble and fall and cut his knee. And it wasn't much of a cut, but he neglected it, and he got blood poisoning in it and within a fortnight he was dead in spite of all the doctor was able to do. And the old man that lived near us always said to me that the noise I heard was the Headless Coach, and that it was the sign that someone was going to get his death in that place. And it was a long time before I plucked up courage enough to go out for turf at night.

27: The Boy who had Knowledge

There was a boy from this side of the country, and he went down the County Limerick working for the farmers there. He hired with a farmer for the year and the farmer was pleased with him. And when Christmas time came the farmer paid him his wages and sent him off home, with a promise that he would come again the next year. And the boy was making his way along. There was no train then, and he was walking on before him. And when the night began to fall he was looking around for a place to stay the night, and he saw the light in a big house away in from the road, and it was a lonely kind of a place without another house in it. And away in with him into the big house, and when he was going in the long avenue a poor travelling man was coming out against him.

'Such a thing,' says the boy to the travelling man, 'do you think there is any chance of a night's lodging in that big house?'

'Didn't I ask the same thing myself, and it was how the woman threatened to set the dog on me. Take my advice, boy, and stay far away from that house!' And the travelling man made off for himself.

But the boy was beginning to get afraid of the dark in the strange place, and he thought he would go into one of the outhouses and stay there until the dawn, whatever.

He went around the back of the outhouses and crept in through the window and up on the loft. And there was a window in the loft and the light from the house shining in through it. And when he looked out he could see the people in the house, a man and a woman. And the woman was laying all sorts of dainties and drinks on the table in front of the man. And the poor boy was hungry, and he couldn't keep his eyes off the fine things on the table.

It was not long until he heard the wheels of a car and the sound of a horse trotting, and in comes the car into the yard, and a man sitting up on it. And you never saw such running around as the pair inside had. The woman swept everything off the table and stuck the things here and there in cupboards and corners, and she opened a big chest and put the man into it. And the next minute she was out the door and great welcome for the man in the car. And the boy began to understand what was up. It was how the fellow inside was a stranger and the man in the car was the real man of the house. And she put up a supper on the table before the man, it wasn't much of a supper, only potatoes and milk.

Well, the boy picked up courage and went to the door and knocked.

'Such a thing, sir,' says he to the man of the house, 'I'm only a working boy making my way home for Christmas, and maybe I'd have your leave to be inside until morning.'

'Come in, and welcome, boy,' says he, 'and draw up to the table with me and eat a bit. I'm having my supper, and indeed it isn't much, but I'm after coming home without being expected, for I thought my business would keep me in the town until morning.'

The boy sat to the table, and he wasn't eating much.

'What sort of work were you doing, boy?' says the man of the house.

'It is working for a farmer I was,' says he, 'and he was thankful to me. I'm from the west and we have great knowledge in the west.'

'What sort of knowledge have you, boy?' says he.

'Great knowledge entirely, Sir, for I can tell where things are hidden. And I think that if you tried that cupboard there, there would be a leg of mutton in it.'

The man of the house didn't believe him, but he looked into the cupboard, and there was a leg of mutton. And the wife after telling him that there was nothing in the house except potatoes and milk.

'And I'd say that there was an apple cake there in that corner behind the churn, and I'd say there was a bottle of whiskey up there on the clevvy.'

And the man of the house found them, and they had a fine supper. And the man of the house was in great admiration of the boy's knowledge.

By this time the wife was gone off to bed, for she was ashamed to stay up with all the things being found. And the man of the house and the boy were sitting one on each side of the fire, talking about this and that. And the man was making excuses that the wife was gone away to bed. 'And I don't like to say anything to herself,' says the man of the house, 'for it is often we don't get along too well together. And with your knowledge, maybe you could tell me what is wrong in this house,' says he.

The boy sat there thinking for a while, and after a time he said, 'You'll excuse me, Sir, but I think there is some bad thing in the house.'

'In the name of God, what sort of a bad thing?' says the man of the house.

'I'm greatly afraid, Sir, that it is the Devil himself that is in it,' says he.

And the farmer was greatly in dread of the whole story. 'Can you do anything for me, boy?' says he.

The boy did nothing except to shove the ends of the poker and the tongs into the fire. 'As soon as they are red, let you do just the same as what I do,' says he in a whisper in the ear of the man of the house.

As soon as they were roasting red the boy whipped out the tongs and the man took the poker, and the boy ran over to the big chest and whipped up the cover and stuck the poker into it. 'Be off out of this house, you Devil!' he bawls as loud as ever he could. And the fellow in the chest ran for his life out the door, and the man of the house and the boy after him. And he was lucky to get away with his life, and he all burned from the poker and the tongs.

Well, when they got up the next morning the wife was as mild as milk. Butter wouldn't melt in her mouth, you'd think. And the man of the house gave the boy five pounds for putting the Devil out of the house, and didn't the woman follow him down the avenue and give him another five pounds when he didn't tell on her.

28: The Funeral Path

I remember one night, a long time ago and I a young fellow, I was out playing cards a good bit from home, and it must be nearly twelve o'clock in the night when I was taking a short cut home over the hill. The first thing I heard was the sound of the feet coming, like people would be marching through the bog after me. And I waited for whoever it was, to see would I have company on the road home.

The next thing I saw was four men coming on after me, with

a coffin on their shoulders, and of course what I thought was that someone was after dying that I did not hear about, and I waited to ask them who it was, for I was sure it was how these men had been sent to bring the coffin from the carpenter so as to have it ready for the funeral. But the men were all strangers to me, and when I gave them 'Good Night', I got no word of an answer from any of them, but to pass me out without taking notice of me.

Well, I got very nervous and I made away home as quick as I could, and went to bed. And the next day I told them about it at home, and my grandmother said that there was an old funeral path there, going out to Templeglantine. But from that day to this, I could not tell you whether the men I saw were from this world or the next, for when I made enquiry around, there was no one buried in Templeglantine around that time.

29: The Coffin

A long time ago, when I was a young lad, I was in a farmer's house below in Monagea one evening and I saw a very strange thing there. It was what looked like a coffin without any cover on it, standing up against the wall, and it had shelves across it like a small cupboard, and there were tins and things in it, the same as you would find on the shelves of a dresser. Well, the old man of the house noticed how curious I was, and he told me about it.

It seems that one night, when he was a young married man, they were sitting around the fire in the kitchen, himself and the wife, and the old people and a few of the neighbouring boys, when the door opened and four men came in with a coffin between them, and they laid it down in the middle of the floor without saying a single word, and then they turned and walked out again. They were strangers to the people in the house. Well, what was in the house of them had not a word to say with the fright; they were staring at the coffin, and they petrified. Well, after a while, the young man of the house plucked up his courage. 'Here, in the name of God,' says he, 'it would be better to see what is inside in it, and to be ready to send for the priest or for the peelers, according to what is there.'

The cover was loose on top of it, and he lifted it up, and the rest of them came around and looked at what was lying inside in it. It was a young girl, and she lying back the same as if she was asleep. 'She is not dead, with that colour on her,' says the old woman, the young man's mother, 'and let ye lift her out of it, and put her down in the bed in the room below.' They did it, and she was breathing away, just the same as if she was asleep. They all stood around the bed watching her, and in about a half an hour she woke up, the same as anyone would wake up out of their sleep. And she was greatly puzzled and very much in dread of them, for she did not know where she was or who all the strangers might be.

Well, the old woman and the young woman hunted the men up into the kitchen, and they started to comfort the poor girl and to tell her that they were respectable people, and that she need not be in dread, that nothing would happen her. And they gave her a drink of hot milk and the like of that to bring back her courage, until finally she told them that she was from near Newtown in County Kerry, and that she was after going to bed, the same as always, at home, and that the next thing she knew was to wake up in this house.

The next day she was a lot better, and they tackled the side-car and started off for Newtown; it was a journey of about fifteen miles to her own place. And when they arrived at her people's place, they found that the whole place was very upset, for when the people of the house were after getting up in the morning three or four days before, they found their daughter, or what they thought was their daughter, dead in her sleep, and they were after waking and burying her. And when she had them persuaded that she was their real daughter, didn't they send a few men to the churchyard to open the grave, and, God between us and all harm, wasn't the coffin in the grave empty.

STORIES FROM MRS MARY MOYLAN

30: The Brown-haired Boy

Once upon a time, a long time ago, there was a boy living with his mother, and she a widow-woman, over there on the side of Rúsca, and they were very poor. A farm is what they had, a cold, hungry patch of the mountain without the feeding of a pair of goats in it, and it is often they were cold and hungry themselves. But they were dragging away, trying to do their best. And one fine day in the early part of the summer, in the middle of May it would be, the boy was above on the top of the hill cutting a bit of turf. And most of the time it was not working he was but looking down at the County Limerick, and the fine farms and the groves of trees. And in the end he could not stand it any more, and he stuck the *sleán* in the bank and off home with him.

'Mother,' says he, 'the garden is planted and a bit of turf cut that will keep you going. And I might as well be off down the County Limerick, to seek my fortune.'

The mother said nothing; she knew he would have to go sooner or later, and all she did was to make up a bag for him with his clean shirt and stockings, and a cake of bastable bread and a bit of boiled fat bacon for the road. And the next morning he got up and dressed himself and said his prayers and ate his breakfast and said goodbye to the old woman and hit the road down into the flat country. 'I'll head for Cashel,' says he, 'for 'tis there the best work is to be got.'

He was a fine, tall, strong boy, with a head of brown hair on him. And the Brown-haired Boy is what everyone used to call him. And he was walking away east all the day, and in the middle of the day he sat alongside a well on the side of the road, and opened up a bag and began to eat his dinner. And with that who did he see but a poor woman hobbling along on a stick. And she asked him for alms.

'Well, my poor woman,' says he, 'I haven't a red copper in

my pocket that I could give you. But you could sit down there near me, and maybe you would like a bit of food.'

And he halved the bread and the bacon with her. And they ate away, conversing about this and that. And when they were finished she looked at him. She hadn't any of the big string of prayers that tramps and beggar women used to have. All she said was: 'God will reward you for what you gave me, and maybe sooner than you expect.' And off with her.

The Brown-haired Boy was walking away until the fall of night. And by that time he was crossing a lonely sort of a place, without a house to be seen. And he sat down under a bush and ate the last of his bread and bacon. And then he fell asleep leaning against the bush. And what did he dream about only the old woman that he gave the bread and bacon to, that she came to him again but that this time she was tall and straight and finely dressed, like an old queen, and that she laid a leather purse at his feet. And when he woke in the morning he was saying to himself that it was a very clear dream, and wondering why he would dream of the stranger and not of his own mother. And he bent down to lace his shoes, and what did he see at his feet but a purse. And he opened it, and there was a golden guinea inside in it. Away with him, walking, and the next town he came to he faced into the hotel and ordered a fine breakfast. And when he paid for the breakfast and told the man to keep sixpence for himself he was putting his change back into the purse, and what did he find in it but another guinea.

'By my hand,' says he, 'but you're the queer sort of a purse.' And he walked on out of the town and when he came to this quiet place he went inside the road ditch and began to draw guineas out of the purse until his pocket was full of them. And there was never more than one guinea in the purse, but the minute he took that one out there was another one in it.

Off home with him as fast as he could travel. And it was slow by him on his feet, and he bought a fine saddle horse from a farmer. And as soon as he came home he gave fistfuls of gold to his mother, enough to keep the poor woman in comfort. God help us, she didn't know was it on her head or her heels she was with all the riches! But nothing would please the Brown-haired Boy but to set himself up as a gentleman. Off with him to the town, and it was the finest clothes and the shiniest boots up to his knees and the best coach that was in the town and six fine horses under it, and a driver up in front and a guard up behind on it and he driving through the country from town to town, spending gold like coppers and great with all the gentry and the rich people. And many is the fine young lady that set her cap at him, but he had no time for them between the driving and the hunting and the sports and the races and all the rest of the pastime he was having.

Until this day he was driving along in his coach somewhere away down the country, when he saw this girl, and the sight of her dazzled his eyes. She was small and fair, and a blue dress on her the same colour as her eyes, and she side-saddle on a white horse, and a man dressed like a servant behind her on a black horse. Out with him out of the coach like a shot, and the next thing was he had a hold of her bridle and he talking up to her. And if he was dazzled with her, she was dazzled with him, and the upshot of it was that he had come with her to see her father, who was the king of that part of the country.

Now this king was a mean old devil, and a clever one, too. And it was not long until he knew all about the Brown-haired Boy, how he was the son of a poor woman, and how he had this purse that was never empty. And he made up to the boy and promised him that he could marry his daughter. And of course the boy was delighted, and so was the girl, for by this time they had a great heart for each other. And the king was taking great notice of the purse, every time he saw it, and what did the old wretch do but to get the harness maker to make another one the very same as it. And then, one night, he asked the Brown-haired Boy to see the purse, and when he had it in his hand he slipped it away and handed the false one to the boy.

The next morning one of the servants in the castle did something for the boy. They were all running to do things for him because it was out with the purse and a guinea here and a guinea there. But this time the purse was empty. Off with him to the old king, and the next thing was that the old king told him to be going, that he wanted no penniless impostors in his

70

castle. And the daughter began to cry and tried to hold onto him, but the king made her go to her own room and told the soldiers to throw the boy out of the castle. But he walked out himself. And they were all sorry to see him going, except the old devil of a king. He had to sell the coach and six horses to pay his servants their wages. And there he was in his fine clothes without a shilling in his pocket. He sold the suit to a tailor for a working man's suit of clothes and a small bit of money. And he bought a shirt and a pair of stockings and a cake of bread and a bit of boiled fat bacon. And there he was, every bit the same as when he left his mother the first time.

Away with him, looking for work. And when he was eating his bread and bacon he couldn't help thinking about the old woman, but there was no sign of her. But that night, when he was stretched out asleep under a hayrick, didn't he dream about her again, that she came to him, and that she was cross with him because he lost the purse.

'It was the king that stole it on you,' says she in the dream, 'and this very minute he is drawing guineas out of it and filling sacks with them. And here is a cloak for you,' says she, 'and the minute you put it around you all you have to do is to say the name of the place, and you'll be standing in that very place.' And she spread the cloak over him.

And when he woke in the morning, there was the cloak. He put it around him.

'The room in the castle where the king is,' says he.

And the next minute he was standing before the king, and the old wretch was drawing one guinea after the other out of the purse, and filling a sack with gold, and the room full of sacks and they clamped like a rick of turf up against the wall. The boy made a sweep for the purse, but the old king was too cute for him. He gave one roar out of him, and in with a crowd of soldiers with swords and spears, and the boy had nothing to do except to jump out the window and it was lucky for him that there was an oak tree growing under the window, for the room was up in the top of the castle. The tree saved him, but the cloak stayed tangled in the branches and the Brown-haired Boy had to run for his life.

He was worse off than ever before now, and that same night he stretched himself out behind a ditch to sleep, cold and hungry. And she came again to him in a dream, but this time she was very angry.

'You foolish boy, I do not know what to do with you,' says she, 'but I'll help you again. This trumpet,' says she, 'will make every soldier that hears it do whatever you tell him,' and she left the trumpet alongside him.

And in the morning there it was sure enough. Back with him to the king's castle. And there was the king drilling his army and all the officers and soldiers marching up and down and wheeling to the right and the left. The Brown-haired Boy blew a blast on the trumpet and the next thing was that all the officers and big men were running to him asking what would they do for him. 'Arrest the king!' says he, and they surrounded the king.

'You have me caught,' says the king, 'and I'll do everything you say. But don't shame me opposite my daughter. Let me put my coat on.'

With that the boy began to look around him to see where the daughter was, for it was a long time since he saw her before. What did the old villain of a king do but to whip up the magic cloak, and the next minute he was on the top of a hill a mile away, and worse than that, going past the boy, and he not to be seen with the speed, he scooped the trumpet out of the boy's hand. Then the old king had every blast on the trumpet, and all the officers and soldiers were running to him to know what he wanted them to do, and it wasn't long until they were running back with their orders to catch the Brown-haired Boy and put him down in the deepest cellar of the castle. But by the time they were halfway back the boy was running for his life. It went hard with him, but he took his feet safe from them in the end.

The time was passing, and the boy was working away as a servant boy for a farmer here and a farmer there, and one evening late didn't he come to the very place where he met the old woman the first time. He sat down, and pulled out his bit of bread and bacon, and says to himself, out loud, 'Ah, if that wise woman was here, wouldn't I give her the half of my bread and my bacon. But, I suppose she would be very cross with me, and the way I lost all to that old king. And my lovely girl. I suppose it was the price of me, and the little sense I had.'

'It was, indeed,' says the voice, and there she was, looking down at him. 'I am very cross with you,' says she, 'but I'll give you the one more chance tomorrow.' She sat alongside him, and he halved the bread and bacon with her and they drank out of the well.

'And now it is time,' says she, 'for me to go and for you to sleep. And when you are going the road tomorrow, a few miles to the east of this place, you'll see an orchard with no house near it. And you'll go into the orchard and take an apple in your left hand and a pear in your right hand, and you'll take a bite of the apple and see what happens, and then you'll take a bite of the pear and see what happens. And then if you don't know what to do about the old king, I can't give you any more help or advice.'

With that she went away and he fell asleep in under a bush. And the birds woke him in the morning, and off he went on his journey, and sure enough it was not long until he came to this orchard and the grandest apples you ever saw, all red, hanging in the trees, and the pears were there too, but they weren't so much to look at at all. So he took an apple in his left hand and a pear in his right hand, and he took a bite of the apple. And the next minute the two eyes got round in his head with the dint of the surprise, for before he could say '*Dia le'm anam*!' wasn't his nose getting longer and longer until it was down on the ground in front of him, and away across the orchard and very nearly out over the ditch and on to the public road before he thought of taking a bite of the pear in his right hand. But with the bite of the pear, the nose got as short as ever it was again. 'By this and by that,' says he, 'but I have the tune now that the old king will dance to.' There was a big clump of white sallies growing in the orchard and he began picking and peeling and twisting and plaiting them until he had the nicest basket made that ever you saw. And he lined it with green ferns and filled it with the reddest of the apples, and away with him walking to the king's castle. And he didn't forget to fill a pocket of his coat with the pears as well.

It was after midday when he came to the castle and he stood outside at the gate, and every call out of him. 'Fine Apples! Fine Apples! Two a penny the fine apples!' so that all that were in the castle heard him. Out with the servant to get the apples for the king, and when he saw them, that they were so fine he ran in with the basket to the king. And the Brown-haired Boy went off into the town, pretending nothing. And the old king was so greedy that his mouth began to water at the sight of the fine red apples, and the next minute he had his teeth in one of them, swallowing lumps of it without giving himself time to chew it. And the next minute to that the king's nose was growing away down on to the floor and away out the door and down the stairs and out into the yard of the castle. It was then that the ructions and the tattarara began, with the king roaring at the top of his voice and the lords and the servants running around and falling over each other, and the king's doctors coming from all sides with their bags full of all kinds of remedies. But they might as well be idle. The nose kept on growing out through the gate and away down the avenue towards the public road. And one of the officers that kept a bit of sense about him told two bands of soldiers to march along on each side of the nose to keep back the people and hunt away the dogs that were trying to bite it. And when it came to the public road they had to stop the cars and the horsemen for fear they would trample it until they had time to lift it up with a plank and two stands so that the people could pass under it. And away across the fields with it and the soldiers always guarding it.

The boy went away into the town and with whatever few shillings he had he bought a tall hat and a swallow tail coat, like a doctor's and a false beard to put over his face, and he did not forget to fill a pocket of the coat with the pears. He was in no hurry at all, and he took it nice and easy going back to the castle. By this time the doctors were all trying their remedies and they were doing no good at all, and the old king was going frantic, for by that time the end of his nose was miles away, and it was not stopping for thorny hedges or furze bushes either, but tearing its way through them and the soldiers doing their best to clear a way for it. And the king was having the heads cut off some of the doctors when they were doing no good and some of them hurting him with the remedies. And then a soldier came galloping up to the castle on a saddle-horse with the message that the nose was nearly coming to the border of the kingdom, and that the king of the next place was waiting for it with all his soldiers and they having spears and swords and hot irons ready, because the next king did not like the old king at all on account of some way he cheated him in the past.

With that a servant came in to say that there was a strange doctor outside that said he could cure the nose. He was let in. Of course it was the Brown-haired Boy, dressed like a doctor.

'I can cure any ailment,' says he, 'but the cure is no good at all unless the sick person has a clear conscience. Now, king, is there anything you have that belongs to another person?'

The king was in a holt and he had to admit it. 'Well, I have a bit of an old purse,' says he, 'that I got the loan of from a young man, and I might have forgotten to give it to him and he leaving the castle.' The purse was brought, and the boy put it in his pocket. He gave the king a bite of the pear, and it was not long until word came that the nose was about a mile shorter. But there it stopped.

'Have you anything else that you shouldn't have?'

'Well, I have an old cloak that I found in the oak tree outside the castle, and it might belong to someone,' said the king. The cloak was brought, and the boy put it around him. He gave him another bite, and word came that the nose was stopped about a mile from the castle this time.

'You must have something else that is not yours,' said the boy.

'Well, there is an old trumpet somewhere around the place that I picked up once and I crossing the castle yard,' says the king. He had to tell the servants to bring it. The boy took it and gave him another bite of the pear, and his nose came back until it was no more than six inches long.

With that the boy turned around to the king's daughter and took off the beard. 'Now you know who you have,' says he.

75

But the daughter gave one shout: 'Take care, my love! Look at the king!'

Hadn't my old devil his sword out and he running to stick the boy! But the boy only gave the one blast on the trumpet, and the next thing was that the soldiers had the old king tied up with ropes. It was glad they were to have the chance at him, on account of his being so hard on them always.

And all the lords and the gentry came together, and they said that the Brown-haired Boy was to marry the king's daughter and to be the king of the country. And they sent the old king to be kept in a castle that was a long way away, and everyone mocking and jeering at the length of his nose. It was the price of him. And the young couple were married, and they sent for the boy's poor old mother, and they lived in peace and plenty from that day to this.

31: The World Under the Ground

Long ago there was a farmer living over alongside the river, and Seán na hAbhann was the name that everyone called him. He was well off until his wife died, and he was left with the one child, a lovely little girl about fifteen years, named Nóirín.

Well, whatever misfortune was down on him, he married again, and that was the woman that wore him down with misery. She was the hard virago, without grace or goodness, and she had a daughter that was as bad as herself, one age to Nóirín. They were doing their best, the two of them, to turn the father against Nóirín with the dint of lies and villainy, but it was no good for them because Seán na hAbhann was so fond of his dead wife's child. When it failed them with the father to get Nóirín put out of the place my two villains thought to get rid of her another way, and one day when she was lifting a bucket of water from the deep well they came behind her and gave her a shove, so that she fell in and sank, and then away home with them, and every screech and *ulagón* out of them, that she was drowned in the well and they not able to save her in time.

Nóirín thought that she was finished with this world for ever, and the water choking her, but where did she come to her senses but lying on a bank of grass in the middle of a meadow with the sun shining and the place all full of flowers. She got up on her feet and walked over to the hedge of the field to see where was she at all. The hedge was so weak with age that it would not hold up a blackbird and when she tried to cross over into the next field, the hedge spoke to her and said: 'Take care! I am old and weak, do not break me!'

'Indeed and I will take care,' says Nóirín, 'I will not touch a twig or a leaf of you,' and with that she jumped right over the hedge without touching it.

'I am thankful to you, girl,' says the hedge, 'and I will make it up to you some day.'

Nóirín was travelling on through the fields until she came to a baker's oven and it going at full heat with a great big fire under it. I tell you that she was surprised when the oven called her.

'Come here, nice little girl, and take out the cakes of bread. I am too hot and I am in dread they will be burnt, for they are baking this last seven years and no one to take them out.'

So she took out the cakes and laid them down on a soft mossy bank.

'May God reward you,' says the oven, 'and good luck to you on your road, and take one of the cakes for fear you would be hungry.'

She took one of the cakes and she was eating it going along.

On she went through the fields and it was not long until she came to where a poor old woman was sitting on a *túrtóg* and she crying with the hunger. It was lucky that she had most of the cake left – it was a very big cake, as round as the top of a forty gallon keg – and she gave a quarter of it to the old woman, and the old woman gave her all the blessings you could think of, and promised to help her if ever she could.

On with Nóirín until she came to a grove of trees, and there was a flock of sparrows there and the poor creatures weak with the hunger.

'What about a small cut of the bread for us,' said the sparrows, 'and we without a full meal for the last seven years.'

'Oh, God help us, you must be starved,' says Nóirín, and she breaking a quarter of the cake out on the ground for them.

'May God reward you,' said the sparrows, 'and if ever we have the chance, you can be sure that we will not forget you.'

She was not long on the road until she came to an apple tree and it bending down with the weight of the ripe apples.

'Will you have pity on me,' says the apple tree, 'and give me a good shake. I am so loaded down with the apples that I am in dread my branches will break.'

She gave the tree a shake, and a right good shake, and a very big load of apples fell down and she made a nice heap of them under the tree.

'May God reward you,' says the tree, 'and I will repay you some day, if I can. But now take as many of the red juicy apples as you like.'

Nóirín took a few of the apples and on she went.

It was not long until she was crossing out over a high ditch when she came on a big ram and his wool tangled in the briers and bushes.

'Girl, dear,' says the ram, 'is there any chance you could shear me. I am tangling in everything and my wool all dirty from dragging along the ground, and I not sheared for the last seven years.'

There was a shears lying on top of the ditch, and it was not long until the ram was sheared.

'I am thankful to you,' says the ram, 'and I hope that some day I will be able to repay you.'

Off with Nóirín again, and what did she see but a cow and her udder trailing on the ground, she had so much milk.

'Would you milk me, little girl?' says the cow, 'I wasn't milked for seven years.'

So Nóirín milked the cow, and the cow promised to repay her some day. It was not long until she met a horse, and his bridle was tangled in a bush.

'Hi, little girl,' says the horse, 'will you untangle my bridle, and I will make it up to you some day.' And she untangled the reins and the bridle so that the horse could go away free.

She was travelling on across the fields until she came to the road, and she was going the road until she came to a little house by the side of it, and it was the only house she could see anywhere, and the night was beginning to fall, so she plucked up her courage and in she went to ask for a night's shelter. There was no one inside but two women, a mother and her daughter, and it would be hard to tell which one of them was the uglier to look at, with teeth like the prongs of a rake on them and yellow skins. The only difference between them was that the old hag had a wispy beard on her like a goat's *meigeal*, and the daughter had not. They gave Nóirín a lump of stale grey bread and a can of water for her supper, and a sop of straw to put under her lying on the ground. But she was hungry and tired, and she ate the bread and slept soundly on the straw.

The next morning when she woke, the women told her that they were the only people living in the World Under the Ground, and that the best thing she could do would be to stay in service with them working as a servant girl, and that she would be well paid for it when she was leaving them at the end of the year. And Nóirín agreed to this, for she had nowhere else to turn.

The next morning she was up at the break of day, and the first thing she had to do was to milk the cows, and that would be no bother to her, and her father having thirty milking cows at home; she was well used to cows. But the minute she was inside the gate of the paddock where the old hag's cows were then they started to run around wild, trying to jump out over the ditch and to puck Nóirín with their horns. The poor girl did not know what to do or where to turn; she was in dread of her life that they would trample her when she heard a voice: 'Open the gate and let me into the paddock!' and there was the cow that she had milked, the cow that was seven years without milking. And Nóirín opened the gate, and that cow was not long quietening the other cows; she had them as tame as day-old lambs in a minute. And Nóirín milked them, and it is she was proud coming back to the house with all the milk. But it was no smile or laugh that the hag or her daughter had for her, for they thought that if they could fault her in her work they could cheat her out of her wages. Nóirín worked away all day, but she got no word of praise or kindness from the women.

The next morning she was up again at the break of day, and the first job she got to do this day was to wash woollen thread, and while she was washing the thread in the stream the old hag came out with two skeins of wool, a short black skein and a long white skein. And she told her that she would have to hold washing them in the stream until the black one changed to white and the white one turned to black. She began, and she held washing them for an hour or more, but she might as well be idle, there was no change coming in the wool. She sat down on the bank and the tears began to come with her, and it would be hard to blame her. But it was not long until she heard a footstep, and when she lifted her head who should be there but the old woman that she gave the share of the cake to.

'Stop your crying now, girl dear,' says the old woman, 'and take your two hanks of wool and draw the white one with the stream and at the same time draw the black one against the stream.'

Nóirín jumped up and did what she was told, and while you would be looking around you the black one was white and the white one was black. Off home to the hag's house with her, and her task done to perfection. And the two women, the hag and her daughter, had eyes as big as saucers on them with the dint of astonishment, but they pretended nothing although they were boiling with rage and disappointment that they could not blame Nóirín or find fault with her.

The next morning as soon as Nóirín had finished whatever scraps they gave her for breakfast, the *cailleach* handed her a sieve and told her to go down to the stream and bring back the full of it with water. Nóirín went off, and she was sitting on the bank and the tears beginning to come with her when a whole flock of small birds flew down and sat on her head and shoulders and her hands. It was the sparrows that she had fed with the bread, and they without a meal for seven years, and they began to sing, and there were words with the song:

> Stuff the sieve with moss
> And plaster it which clay,

And then you can take
The water away.

That was enough for Nóirín. She stuffed moss into the holes in
the sieve and plastered it nicely with yellow clay, and home
with her and the sieve full to the brim of water. And if the
women were disappointed the day before, they were mad with
the rage today, but they still pretended nothing, only watched
their chance to cheat her.

It went on like that, the women giving her hard tasks to do,
and she doing them with the help of her friends, until at last the
patience broke on the hag and her daughter, and they told
Nóirín to take her wages and be off with herself. And she was
to take her wages like this; she was to go into the room and
there were three caskets on the table, a beautiful gold casket,
and a fine silver casket and a dirty little lead casket. And before
Nóirín could put her hand on any one of them, she heard this
fluttering at the window, and there were the sparrows:

Leave the gold
And leave the silver.
But take the lead,
And you'll be saved.

That was the song they had at the window. So Nóirín took the
lead casket and put it under her shawl, and away with her,
making back along the way she came to the house the first day.
But it was not long until she heard the screeching and the calling behind her, for the hag and her daughter saw the gold and
the silver caskets left behind, and the lead casket gone, and
after her with them and sparks from their heels. Nóirín was
running for her life, but they were overtaking her when who
did she see but the cow that was not milked for seven years.

'Come here behind me,' says the cow, 'and I'll put them
astray.' And when the women came up the cow called to them:
'Over that ditch and away with her,' and the women cleared the
ditch in one leap and off with them in the other direction. On
with Nóirín then, but it was not long again until they were on
her track again, and she was gasping for breath with the dint of

the running when she heard the call – 'In under the heap of wool with you, girl!' and there was the ram and the seven years' growth of wool in one big heap alongside him. In under the wool with Nóirín and away with the two women again and sparks from their heels.

On with Nóirín again and this time she got as far as the apple tree and the big heap of apples under it. And the horse that she had freed and he grazing under the tree. 'In under the apples with you!' says the tree, and the horse worked the hooves on the heap until she was well covered. It was not a minute until the women were there again and 'Where is she? where is she?' out of them.

'It is up in that tree she is,' says the horse, and away up the apple tree with them, but the tree moved the branches so that it was easy for them to climb up but very hard for them to come down, and by the time they were on the ground, Nóirín was gone a good bit of the road. The next thing she came to was the hedge, and she in dread that she would never be able to jump it. But the hedge opened a gap when she was coming up and closed up again just when the two hags were going through it. And it was full of all sorts of briers and bushes, and by the time they tore themselves out of the hedge it was nightfall, and they were all raggedy and torn from the thorns and the briers. So they went away home, and they were not in any nice temper. But by that time Nóirín was at the very spot where she had landed when she fell down the well, and she was so tired and worn out that she fell down dead asleep. And when she opened her eyes again where did she find herself but lying alongside the well near her father's house. And the lead casket was safe alongside her hand.

Off home with her running, and the first person she met was her father. And wasn't he delighted to see her, and he thinking she was drowned in the well, according to the story of the stepmother. But it was the sour face the stepmother had before her, and the scolding and the screeching, so that in the end Nóirín could not stand it any more, and she told her father that she was going to live in a little cabin that they had down the fields. And she spent a good part of the day sweeping and cleaning the little cabin. And in the evening she thought of the lead casket, and she opened it. It was then that the eyes opened on her, for it was so full of gold and jewels that the shine of it nearly blinded her. And as fast as she took anything out of it, it was full again. She was drawing gold and jewels and money, and silk carpets and curtains and clothes out of it until she had the cabin shining like a palace.

There was one of the neighbours crossing the field, and he wondered to see the smoke from the chimney of the cabin, and over with him to see who was there. He was so blinded by all the wealth that he did not recognise Nóirín, and what he told everyone was that a queen was after coming to live in the cabin, and that she had a palace made of it. And they were all coming to see the queen, and Nóirín made them all welcome, for there was food and drink in plenty coming from the lead casket, too. And Nóirín told them all how she was in the World Under the Ground, and how she got the riches and escaped from the hags. And when the stepmother and daughter heard about it, they made up the plan to get riches for themselves too. The stepmother wanted the daughter to go and the daughter wanted her mother to go, until finally, and they arguing and fighting at the brink of the well, the old woman gave the daughter a shove, and away down with her.

She came to herself, the same as Nóirín, but it was not the same as Nóirín she conducted herself. She broke down the hedge and laughed at the oven that was full of bread. She threw stones at the sparrows and made fun of the apple tree and the horse and the ram and the cow. When she came to the house of the old hag and the daughter she was full of talk of all she was going to do for them. You would think that she was going to work all round her, but it was not long until the two hags were well tired of her, she was so lazy and so slovenly. And if they were not satisfied with a neat little girl like Nóirín, it would be hard for them to have anything to do with a *straoil* like this one. And finally they took her into the room, and showed her the two caskets that Nóirín left behind her. And nothing would do her but to take the gold casket. And the hags let her go, but they gave her a good beating first. And she had no easy journey home, for the cow pucked her and the ram hit her, and the horse kicked her and the tree let down a big load of hard green apples on top of her, and the birds pecked her and pulled wisps out of her hair, and it like a bush by this time, and finally, when she came to the hedge she was half the day tearing herself through it.

Finally she came to the place under the well, and she threw herself down and fell asleep, and she woke up alongside the well and her mother waiting for her. And away home with the two of them; they could not wait to open the casket. But it is they were sorry they ever opened it, for what came out but frogs and lizards and serpents and every kind of crawling thing: and away with them running mad through the country and they screeching at the top of their voices, and the creepy-crawlies after them. And that was the last that anyone ever saw of them.

Nóirín and her father settled down in the old home, and they had it like a palace with all the things out of the lead casket, and they without a trouble in the world, except for the number of visitors that were coming to see all the grand things. And it was not long until the son of the king came to see all the grand things, and when he saw Nóirín nothing would do him but to make a match with her. And they were married, and what was in the country of people came to the wedding. And if they were not happy, it was no fault of Nóirín's.

32: The Tailor of Rathkeale

There was a little tailor once upon a time in the town of Rathkeale, a small weak little man like a lot of the tailors of his time. He was working away at his trade, but he was never satisfied with it and always saying to himself what a great fellow he would be if he only got a chance. And the neighbours used to joke him about it. Well, it happened one day when he sat down to his dinner, to a big bowl of porridge, that there was a great cloud of flies and midges flying around his head and perching on the table and on the porridge. And the tailor – his name was Jack – hated flies and midges, and he made a slash with the wooden spoon that he had eating the stirabout and he hit a whole lot of flies and midges. The next thing he did was to start counting how many of them he had killed, and he made out that he had seventy of them dead. 'That is three score and ten,' says Jack, 'and it is the great man that would kill three score and ten at one blow!'

Well, he started boasting about it among the neighbours, and before long the prime boys were all praising him up to the moon for his great deed, so that his head was turned by all the flattery. What did he do but go to the blacksmith and tell him to make a sword. And when it was made, the blacksmith was told to write along the blade: 'Three score and ten at every blow.' And away with Jack, sword and all, to seek his fortune.

He was travelling before him a very long distance until finally he came to a great big castle. He asked who lived there, and they told him it was the king of Ireland, and that this king had great need of brave fighting men. And nothing would do the tailor but to face up to the gate of the castle with the sword in his hand so that everybody could read what was written on it. And the soldiers at the gate were half afraid of the little man with the big sword. And when they read what was written on the blade of the sword, they sent word in to the king to come out and see this great warrior. And the king invited Jack to come into the castle and sit down to the table alongside him to eat his dinner. And after a while of talking about the weather and the crops, the king drew down the question of the sword.

'You seem to be a brave fighting man,' says the king.

'Ah, no!' says Jack, 'but one of the worst men that ever left the town of Rathkeale.'

And the king began to tell all his troubles to Jack. He was building a new castle, and the builders could make no progress, for what they built during the day was always thrown down the same night. And he put soldiers to guard it, but when he came in the morning some of the soldiers were dead and the rest of them after running away, and he did not know what was doing the damage. 'And maybe,' says he to Jack, 'you would stay

85

up a night at the castle, you are such a brave man. And maybe you won't be able to beat whatever it is that is knocking my castle, but at least you will be able to tell what kind of a monster is doing the damage.'

They made a bargain. Jack would watch the castle for the night, and when he brought the word to the king in the morning he would get fifty pounds.

Well Jack, being a small little man, was able to hide himself in a place where no ordinary man would fit. And where he hid himself was up in the fork of a tree. Out in the night he heard this great noise coming, and what was it but three big giants with sledge-hammers.

'It is built again tonight,' says one of them, 'and it is spoiling the view on us and on our mother. Come on, lads, and we'll knock it.'

'Easy with that sledge,' says the second giant, 'and take care not to hit me with it like you did last night, or you'll earn it!'

'Hold your tongues,' says the third one, 'you are doing nothing but talking. Go on now, and knock it.' And one of them made a swing of the sledge, and with that Jack aimed with a paving stone and hit the second one.

'Didn't I tell you not to hit me?' says he. 'And I won't warn you again.'

It was no good for the first fellow to be denying it; he would not listen to any reason. Finally, they turned to the castle again, and if they did, Jack met the second fellow with another paving stone. He did nothing but swing the sledge on his brother and stretch him dead on the ground. The third giant was inclined to argue, but the second giant roared at him that that is what would happen to him as well as to the brother if he did not leave him alone. And away home with them, quarrelling and arguing. Jack came down and after a lot of slashing and sawing with the sword he got the head off of the giant and dragged it along with him, he was not able to lift it, to the king's door. The king was greatly pleased, and praised Jack to the skies, and it was not fifty pounds he gave him but a hundred. 'And maybe,' says the king, 'that you will stay up and mind the castle again tonight.' And they made the bargain, for a hundred pounds this night.

So Jack was up in the tree again by the fall of dark, and a good supply of paving stones in a bag by him. And it was not long until the giants came and began to level the castle. Jack aimed a stone, the same as the night before. And the row started between the giants, and you can be sure that Jack helped it on as well as he could.

'Stop your annoying me now,' says one of the giants, 'and let you remember what happened to the other fellow last night, because I would do for you as quick as I did for him.'

With that, Jack met the other giant with a big stone. 'Who is starting the trouble now?' says the giant that was hit, 'or who is hitting who?' With that the row rose in earnest between them, and before it was over one of them was stretched dead on the ground, and his head split with the sledge-hammer. Away home with the giant who was still living, and down with Jack out of the tree, and cut off the dead giant's head and away with him back to the king's castle, dragging the head after him, and I can tell you he had enough to do to bring it.

Of course the king was delighted. 'Oh Jack,' says he, 'what is written on your sword isn't a word of a lie. And maybe you would go the third night and finish off the third giant, as you are about it.' And it was not a hundred pounds he gave him for the second night's work, but two hundred. And he promised him the same amount for the third night.

Off with Jack at the fall of night, and up on the tree the same as before. And when the giant came, Jack met him with a big rock in the side of the head. 'Are the two of you there again, up to your old tricks?' says the giant, thinking it was the two brothers.

'Indeed it is not the two of them, but me,' says Jack.

'And who might you be, little man?' says the giant.

'Don't mind your "little man" to me,' says Jack, 'but go over there behind the castle, and you'll see what happened to your two brothers when they got cheeky with me!'

The giant was a simple sort of a fellow, and over he went and looked at the corpses of the two brothers, and no heads on them. 'Where are their heads, little man?' says he.

'Don't mind your "little man" to me!' says Jack, 'but look at my sword and you will see what kind of man I am.'

The giant read what was on the sword, and he got very much in dread. 'Oh sir, do not kill me, but come home with me and explain to my mother what happened to the two brothers, for she is blaming me for it,' says he.

Well and good, Jack consented to come home with him. And when they came to the giant's house, inside in a big wood, and the mother was there, a frightful looking old hag; she had two big long teeth sticking down out of her jaw like the handles of two sweeping brushes, and, by the same token, not another tooth in her head, but every time she talked her nose and her chin were hitting off each other, making a noise like a *bodhrán*.

So Jack told her that it was himself that killed the two giants. But would she believe him?

'A little *caistín* of a man like you to kill my two big sons!' says she. 'It is tricks, that is what it is!' But the third son would not believe her; he was greatly in dread of Jack all the time.

She started to make the supper. 'Son,' says she to the giant, 'there isn't a bit of meat in the house. Will you get a bit somewhere for the supper?' Off with the giant, and Jack along with him, to the king's fields, where there was a big herd of fine bullocks. The giant caught one of them and twisted his neck. 'You do the same now, Jack, and we will have enough for this evening,' says he. But Jack drove all the bullocks into the corner of the field.

'What I am going to do,' says he, 'is to take them all, and we won't have to be coming back every day for them.'

'Oh, no, Jack,' says the giant, 'the meat would go bad on us. Two of them is plenty,' and he picked up the second bullock and off home with them. The giant was boasting to his mother what a great man Jack was, how he was going to kill the whole herd of bullocks, but the mother was trying to persuade him that Jack was only making a fool of him.

'But, look here,' says she, 'there isn't a bit of firing in the house to boil the supper. Let you go out and gather a handful of *brosna* for me.'

Off with the two of them out into the wood, and the giant pulled up a big dead tree by the roots. 'Let you pull another one, and we have enough, Jack,' says he.

But that wouldn't satisfy Jack. He got a bit of rope and started to run through the wood with it. 'I'll tear up the whole wood,' says he, 'and then we will not have to be gathering twigs for the fire every day.'

'Oh, no, Jack,' says the giant, 'for if you tear up the whole wood, everyone will see where our house is, and I want to keep it hidden.' And with that he pulled up the second tree and away home with them. The giant boasted greatly about what a strong man Jack was, but the old hag would not believe a word of it.

She started to make the supper in a big pot. 'Will you have enough in the two bullocks, men?' says she.

'And sure we will,' says Jack, 'one bullock apiece is not bad feeding.' The giant was getting more in dread than ever, when he heard the big appetite the small man had, and he hardly able to finish one bullock for his supper of an evening.

'Let you go out, the two of you, and have sport for yourselves while the supper is boiling,' says the old hag. Out with them into the yard. There was a blacksmith's anvil lying in the yard, a lot bigger than the anvil you would see at the forge. The giant picked it up in one hand. 'This is a little game that my brothers and myself used to play,' says he. And he tossed the anvil over the top of the house, the same as you might toss your cap in the air. And he ran around the house and caught the anvil before it touched the ground. 'Now, Jack, it is your turn,' says he.

Jack took off his coat and trussed up his sleeves. 'Stand back, and give a run at it,' says he, 'and I'll fling it from here to County Limerick. It will come in handy for my poor old mother, to iron the clothes with. It is the stone of a mill she was using when I left home, and it was getting a bit heavy for her, the creature.' But when the giant heard that he wouldn't have it at all; he did not want to lose the anvil. And he had great boasting to the mother about how strong Jack was. But she was saying all the time that Jack was making a fool of him.

Well, the supper was ready, and the mother put a boiled bullock up before each of them. And Jack made some excuse to go out for a minute, and what did he do but to fold the skin of one of the bullocks like a bag, and put it inside his shirt. And it was into the skin that he put most of the meat, until he had the table cleared in front of him. And he would not be satisfied until the giant gave him a quarter of his own bullock, and into the bag with that too.

'And now, my brave giant,' says Jack, 'I must show you the way to cure yourself of a surfeit of boiled meat,' says he, and with that he picked up the carving knife and ripped up the skin, and out with all the meat around the floor. And before the mother could stop him, the giant had himself split up the middle, trying to be as good as Jack. And down with him in a heap on the floor, stone dead. And the old hag let out a screech out of her that nearly split the roof, and away with her running mad thróugh the country and was never heard of again.

But Jack cut the head off the giant, and dragged it away back to the king and told him that the danger was over for good and all. And the king was so delighted that he gave Jack a thousand pounds this time, all gold, in a bag, and a horse to carry himself and all the wealth home to his old mother in the town of Rathkeale. And he minded his money, and never had a day's want for the rest of his life.

33: King Whiskers

There was a king in Ireland once upon a time, and he was very rich and powerful, and all the other kings were afraid of him, and they used to send him presents to pacify him. He had everything his own way except in one thing. His wife was dead a while, and he had only the one child, a daughter, and what was coming against him was the daughter's contrariness, for she wouldn't be said nor led by him in anything. No sooner had he a thing said than she would have the very opposite to say, and as for taking his advice, if he said she had a right to do this, it was the direct contrary that she would do. He was persecuted from her. And you wouldn't mind if she had any bad in her, but she hadn't. She was the most beautiful princess that ever was seen, and as for managing a house or castle for that matter, there wasn't her equal in the whole of Ireland.

Well, the king was saying to himself that she should be thinking of getting married. And, with Shrove coming on, he was asking this prince and that great lord to come and visit him, to see if she would take a fancy to any of them. But no, she was so contrary that it was how she was making mockery and fun of them, and they as handsome a crowd of young noblemen as you could wish to see. Finally the king gave a big party, and the biggest hall in the castle was crowded with hundreds of people, gentle and simple, all enjoying themselves with music and dancing and every abundance of food and drink.

It was getting on in the night, and the enjoyment was at its height, when the king stood up and called for silence. And he made a speech, saying that there were several kings' sons and great princes and wealthy lords in the company, and that now he was asking his daughter to go amongst them and pick out the man she would marry. And she started to make a laugh of them in front of the whole company. She came to the first one and he was a fine, big stout young man. 'I wouldn't marry a barrel of lard!' says she.

She came to the next man, a great tall fellow, a prince from some foreign country. 'And I wouldn't marry a telegraph-pole,' says she.

The next one was from Spain, or somewhere like that, and he had a very dark complexion. 'Is it to marry a sooty-face like that?' says she, and the crowd were in stitches of laughing to see the disappointment on the faces of the princes and the nobles.

And so on, through the whole lot of them. One of them was pale, and she called him Whitewash, and another one of them was a bit short of hair and she called him Baldy, and another boy, that was blushing with shyness, and it would be hard to blame him, well, she called him Furnace.

And the last of them all, when she came to him her heart nearly stopped, for he was the finest and noblest looking man she ever saw in her life, tall and handsome, with a beautiful head of golden hair and a beard of the same colour, trimmed in the latest fashion, and he all dressed in silk and satin and jewels. She would greatly like to say that she would marry him, but the

Devil was pinching her all the time to go against the father, and what did she say but: 'And I wouldn't marry you, old Whiskers!'

Well, the old king was so mad he was fit to be tied. He kept his temper, anyway, until he had said good night to the company and sent them all home. It was then that he turned to the daughter, and he in a fearful rage.

'Now, my lady,' says he, 'this is enough of this kind of a carry on. I'm tired of it,' says he, 'and if you won't choose a man from the finest nobles and princes of all the kingdoms, I'll choose one for you. And this is what I'll do. The first tinker or travelling man that comes to the door, I'll marry you to him! And that might teach you manners! Off to bed with you now, without a word out of you,' says he, for he could see that she was gathering herself for speech, 'or it is how I'll do what I should have done long ago, and that is to take a strap to you!'

Well, she was properly frightened, and she slipped off to bed for herself.

The very next day, who should come up to the door, but a great big ragged fellow, with black hair and a bushy beard, and a tinker's budget on his back, and strings of cans and saucepans around his neck. 'Here is the very man,' says the king, and went out and ordered the tinker to be brought in to the main room of the castle. And he sent for the bishop, no less, and in spite of all her crying and bawling the princess was married to the big tinker. And when they were married, the king didn't even say a word to her, but only put his hand down in his pocket and pulled out a handful of money. 'Here now, my man, is ten pounds for you. That is all the fortune she will get, for she is so contrary that she doesn't deserve any more. And take her away out of my sight now, and don't let me see either of you again until you have manners put on her.' Away with them, and she still bawling and crying.

But the tinker turned out to be a quiet, mannerly kind of a fellow that didn't abuse or ill-treat her, and after a while she dried her tears and started to make a bit of conversation with him. They were passing through a fine part of the country, with grand crops of wheat and oats, and she remarked on them. 'Oh, yes,' says he, 'all the fields there belong to King Whiskers, and by the same token, he is the one you said you wouldn't marry yesterday.'

It was the same with a lake that they came to, full of all kinds of fish and a forest full of all kinds of game, and grand farms and villages and towns – they all belonged to King Whiskers, for by this time they were out of her father's part of the country and going through the neighbouring kingdom. And she was beginning to regret greatly that she didn't marry King Whiskers when she had the chance. And she began to cry and bawl again, and the tinker was trying to pacify her, but he might as well be idle.

Well, coming on towards nightfall, and they after walking all day, they came to this little *bothán* on the side of the road. 'Well,' says the tinker, 'here we are home at last. And you start making the supper,' says he, 'while I'm reddening the fire.'

She had to wash the handful of potatoes that he was after gathering in the course of the day, a few here and a few there, and put them down in a pot over the fire. And it was no great practice she ever had with the like, but always waited on hand and foot. He sat down and ate his supper, but she couldn't touch a thing, she had so little appetite for anything

The next day he gave her an old dress to put on instead of her own fine one. 'What will you do,' says he, 'to help us to gather a bite and a sup?' He was greatly afraid that she hadn't much experience of any kind of work. And of course he was right, she was hardly able to do a hand's turn at any kind of work, except a bit of fine embroidery or painting, and that is no great advantage to a tinker's wife.

Finally what he hit upon was to send her into the city and to set up a stall there on market days and sell the tins and saucepans and the baskets that he would make, as well as old chaneys and other little things that he would gather through the country. So he went into the market with her and set her up in the stall, and she was trying to make a hand of selling things, until a herd of cows came down the street, and the fellow in charge of them was very drunk, and where did he drive them but in through her stall, and made flitters of everything she had.

Home with her to the tinker, and she crying her eyes out. And, faith, he didn't abuse her or anything, but just to shake his head. 'I'm greatly in dread that you'll never make a market dealer,' says he, 'and the only thing for it is for you to go in service. Here,' says he, 'you have some experience of a palace. We will go up to King Whiskers' palace and get employment for you there.' Up with them to the palace and she hiding her face with shame. Well, the head cook said they wanted a girl to wash up the pots and pans, and that she could start work straight away.

And there she was every day in the scullery of the palace, scrubbing the pots and the pans, and every night the cook used to give her a bag full of the bits of meat and puddings and cakes and so on that were left after the dinner. And she was glad to have them because it was often the tinker came home empty-handed after the day.

Well, a day came, whatever, when there was great *rí-rá* in the palace, and all the servants running around and preparing this and that and getting everything ready. It was announced that King Whiskers would be getting married the very next day to a strange princess. There was great excitement, and such laying of tables and setting out of food and drink as you never saw before. And, of course, there were heaps of pots and pans to be cleaned and scrubbed, and it was late before the poor girl had them finished, and she was all soot and grease from them. The cook says to her: 'Slip in there now to the banquet hall, and fill your pockets with the cakes and puddings, for you will be hungry enough going home, and maybe your husband won't have anything gathered during the day.'

In with her, and she filling her pockets with a bit from this and a bit from that. And the next thing was that the big doors opened and in came the whole company of nobles and big people, and King Whiskers at the head of them. She nearly went down through the ground with shame.

'Who have we here?' says the king. 'Is it a thief we have? Well, she will have to dance for her supper, whoever she is!' And he told the musicians to strike up and ordered her out on the floor to dance the best she could. Well, she did her best, and indeed she was a good dancer, but with every hop and step bits of cake and puddings and legs of chickens were flying out of her pockets. And the whole crowd were splitting their sides laughing at her.

Then King Whiskers stood up and called for silence. 'This girl,' says he, 'is the princess from the next kingdom. And when I went to ask her to marry me, it was how she made a mock of me before the whole palace. And I wasn't the only one, for there were princes and fine gentlemen from near and far, and she jeered at them all and insulted them. And now she knows what it is to be made a mockery of,' says he. 'But there is one thing she does not know, and that is that she is my wife and the new queen of this country, and the people that are laughing at her now will be bowing down before her tomorrow. It was I was the tinker that got her in marriage from her father. And even though it was a hard thing for a princess to be married to a tinker, she did her best to please me. She was proud before, but she is not proud any more.'

Three or four fine ladies came up to her and brought her away to a room in the palace and took off her dirty clothes and dressed her in silks and satins and jewels, and then they brought her back and put her sitting alongside her husband, and the celebrations of the wedding began, and for all I ever heard they might be going on still.

34: Máirín Rua

There was a well-to-do farmer and his wife one time in a certain part of the country and they had everything they wanted. And they were expecting their first child. And one day an old woman came to the door for alms, and the wife gave her out whatever she had and welcome. 'Your child will be a daughter, and she will be beautiful,' says the old woman. Time passed, and the little girl was born, and she was a lovely child.

Some time after that again, the wife was expecting another child. And the old travelling woman came again to the door, and when the wife handed out whatever she had to her, the old woman said the same thing. 'Your child will be a daughter, and she will be beautiful.' And it happened like that; the child was born and she would be more beautiful than the first if that same was possible.

Well, the years were going past, and the two little girls were getting more handsome every day. And the wife was expecting another child. And the old travelling woman came again, but whatever happened this time, the woman of the house was very short with her, and the old woman was not pleased at all. 'Your child will be a daughter, and she will be ugly. And ugly she will stay until some young man marries her for herself and not for her appearance.'

Well, God bless the mark, when the third child was born she had a head of red hair, and a beard of the same colour growing on her face.

According as they were growing up, the two eldest girls, the good-looking ones, were always dressing up and looking at themselves in the glass, and putting jewels and ribbons on themselves. And the youngest one – her name was Máirín Rua on account of the red hair – she only got very poor clothes and she had to do all the sweeping and cleaning while the sisters were enjoying themselves. And they hardly would talk to her. And when there were strangers around they pretended not to know her at all.

Well, time was passing until what happened but the father to get sick and die. And he left them in a bad way, very poor. And the mother did not know what to do, until one day the eldest daughter said that there was nothing for it but to go and seek their fortune out in the world. And they agreed to that. The mother started to make cakes for them for the journey, but she hadn't much flour. Says she to the first girl, 'Will you take half a cake with my blessing or the whole cake without it?'

'I'll take the whole cake,' says she, 'for your blessing would not keep away the hunger.' And she took the whole cake.

The mother faced the second daughter and put the same question. And she took a whole cake too. But when it came to Máirín Rua's turn, she said the half of the cake would do her fine, if she got the mother's blessing with it.

Well, they started out, and as soon as they got out of the mother's sight, the two eldest started to do everything they could to leave Máirín Rua behind. They tied her to a tree, and by the time they were at the next cross-roads there she was waiting for them. They threw her down in the bog, and clamped the turf on top of her, and it was the same story. Finally, they tied a big rock to her neck and shoved her into a big lake, but they weren't gone a mile, when she was out in front of them again. So they decided they would have to put up with her.

It was coming on to nightfall, and they saw a great big castle, full of lights, alongside the lake, and they went up to the door and asked to be inside from the dark. And they got lodgings. But who should be living in that castle but a giant and his wife and his three daughters. They were put to sleep in the same room as the daughters, the giant's children in one bed and our own three in the other bed. Well, Máirín Rua gave her sisters a nudge when the other three were gone asleep. 'Watch me now,' says she, 'and do what I say. For I am greatly in dread that the giant and his wife will be up to some villainy.' And she made them get up and move their bed into the far corner of the room, and, what was more, she took the three nightcaps off the heads of the giant's children and put them on their own.

It was not long until they heard the giant and his wife coming. 'Take care, now,' says the giant's wife, in a whisper, 'and be sure you find the right bed. It is the nearest to the door, and they have no caps on.' The giant was feeling around the room. 'I have them now,' says he, 'these have no caps and they are the nearest to the door.' And he took out his knife and killed the three in the bed. 'We'll have a fine supper tomorrow night,' says he, 'when one of them is boiled and the second one fried and the third one roasted.' The minute they were out of the room, away with Máirín Rua and the sisters, as fast as they could travel.

Well, they travelled on until they came to a big town where the king had his palace. And this king had three sons. And when the first son saw the first sister, he said that he would marry her, she was so beautiful. And when the second son saw the second sister he wanted to marry her, she was so beautiful. But when the third son saw the red beard on Máirín Rua, he wasn't a bit anxious to marry her.

And nothing would do the two eldest sons, but that their father should ask the girls to dinner with them, and while they were at dinner, the girls told the king how clever Máirín Rua was, to save them from the giant. 'That giant is a great enemy of mine,' says the king, 'and if you bring me his magic cloak of invisibility, my eldest son will marry your eldest sister.' So Máirín Rua agreed, and away with her the next night back to the giant's castle. The giant had the cloak spread over the bed where himself and the wife were asleep, and Máirín whipped it off the bed and around her. And once it was around her, she could not be seen. And away with her, as fast as she could run, back to the king's palace. The king was delighted.

That same night, when they were all eating their dinner, the king himself drew down the story of how clever Máirín Rua was, and how easily she bested the giant. 'That giant has a sword of light,' says he, 'that shines in the dark like a lighthouse. And if you bring me that sword of light, my second son will marry your second sister.' She agreed to venture it that same night. Back with her to the giant's castle. That was not so easy, because it would be hard to hide a sword of light, with all the blaze coming from it. But she thought of a plan.

What she did was to get a great big bag of salt, and to climb up to the top of the castle. And when the giant's wife was making the soup for the supper, for every pinch of salt the wife put in, Máirín Rua let fistfuls of it fall down the chimney into the soup. The giant was grumbling greatly when he was having the supper, making out there was too much salt in it, but the wife wouldn't hear of that, and she made him finish it. And, signs be on it, he couldn't sleep with the drought, for the salt made him frightfully thirsty. 'Reach me a drink of water,' says he.

'There is not a drop in the house,' says she. 'Go out and bring a bucket of it from the well,' says he, 'and it is the price of you to have to go, with all the salt you put in the soup.' Nothing would do him but that she must go, and in the end she got up and got the bucket, to pacify him.

'It is as black as pitch,' says she, 'and how will I find my way to the well?'

'Can't you take the sword of light,' says he, 'and the path will be as bright as day.'

So she took the sword of light and held it up to show her where to go. And when she came to the well, she laid it to one side so that she could work the windlass. And the minute she did, Máirín Rua had snapped it up, and away with her. And the old king was delighted, and that very evening, at the dinner, he drew down the matter again. 'That giant,' says he, 'has a pair of seven-league boots, and if I could get that pair of boots, my youngest son would marry you.' By this time the youngest son had a great admiration for her, in spite of being so ugly, because she was so brave and clever, and so good to the sisters.

Well, she crept into the giant's castle that night again and she took up the giant's boots and put her feet into them. With that the giant woke up and came after her. 'Ha ha!' says he, 'my fine lady, I have you now. What a fool I would be not to keep my seven-league boots locked in that chest there from the likes of you!' He caught her by the hair of the head and shoved her into a big sack. 'What I'll do now,' says he, 'is to hang this sack up to the rafters. And then I'll go to the wood and cut the biggest stick I can find. And then, my fine lady,' says he, 'I'll make snuff out of you with the beating I'll give you!' So he tied the sack up to the rafters, and away with him to the wood, with a big hatchet, to cut the biggest stick he could find.

Well, the giant's wife was asleep in her bed, and what woke her was to hear laughing and singing in the kitchen. 'What is going on here?' says she, 'or what are you laughing and singing about, whoever you are, inside in the bag?'

'I'm laughing and singing because I am so delighted to be going to Heaven,' says the voice inside the bag.

'And could I go to Heaven in that old bag?' says the wife, 'because I am getting a bit tired of himself.'

'You could so,' says the voice, 'but to let me out and go in yourself. But you will not get the chance free,' says she, 'you will have to give me a bag of gold.'

The foolish woman gave her the bag of gold and went into

the bag herself. And no sooner was she tied up to the rafter but Máirín Rua had the boots whipped up out of the chest, and away with her.

The giant couldn't make it out when he heard the singing inside the sack. He gave it a wallop of the stick. The wife began to scream, and he knew the tone of her voice. He opened the bag and heard the story and away with him after Máirín, but when he came to a big wide river, he forgot he hadn't the seven-league boots on him, and he tried to jump it. And it was into the middle of it he went, and he was drowned.

Well, there was great rejoicing when she got back to the palace, and the king said that the three couples should be married then and there. And as soon as they were married, and the young prince turned to Máirín Rua, wasn't the hair gone from her face, and wasn't she even more beautiful looking than either of her handsome sisters. And they all lived happily ever after.

35: The Twelve Swans

Once upon a time there was a king and a queen living in a castle in a certain part of Ireland. They were rich and powerful and they had everything they could wish for. Except for one thing, for they had twelve sons, twelve of the finest young men that were ever seen, but they had no little girl. And the queen was always hoping for a daughter, and she was very sad and disappointed when there was no girl. And one day in the winter time, when she was sitting up at her window looking out at the country all covered with snow, she saw her sons out hunting in the fields near the castle. And one of them shot a raven, and the raven flew a bit and fell down in the yard of the castle just under the queen's window. When the queen saw the raven bleeding on the snow she said to herself: 'Oh, aren't they three lovely colours, the red, the white and black. And if I only had a little girl coloured like that, with black hair and white skin and red lips, isn't I that would be happy!' And she got so sad, thinking about the daughter, that she said to herself: 'And I would give anything in the world to have a little girl like that. I would give every one of my twelve sons to have a little girl.'

The next thing was that she heard someone behind her, and when she turned around, there was an old woman standing in the room, and she did not know how the old woman could be there, because there was only one stairs to the room, and a soldier always on guard minding it.

'You have a great wish for a daughter?' says the old woman.

'I have, indeed, a great wish,' says the queen.

'And you would give anything in the world, even your twelve fine sons to have a daughter?'

'I would, so,' says the queen.

'Then,' says the old hag, 'it will be done as you wish,' and with that she vanished.

And so it happened. Before very long a beautiful little daughter was born to the king and the queen. But the minute the baby was put in the cradle and the twelve sons let in to see her, they all turned into white swans and the whole twelve of them flew out the window and away. The king and the queen and everyone in the castle and the country were all greatly troubled by this, and there was great mourning for the twelve sons of the king. But there was nothing they could do. The mother knew well what had happened, that the old hag had taken the sons away under enchantment in exchange for the daughter, but she was afraid to say anything about it to the king or anyone else.

The little girl was growing up very clever and very beautiful, with hair as black as the raven, skin as white as the snow and lips as red as blood. And when she was sixteen years old there were many princes from neighbouring kingdoms and from kingdoms far away coming to ask her hand in marriage. But her parents thought she was a bit young yet. There was one thing troubling her, for she often noticed her mother sitting in her room crying to herself. And one day she asked her mother, what was she crying for, and why was she always so sad, and the mother told her the whole story, how the brothers were changed into swans. And the girl made up her mind that she would go looking for her brothers far and near until she found them.

She got her things ready and she started off, asking along the road of everyone she met for news of the twelve swans. And finally she came to a part of the country where they told her about a lake with a castle alongside it, and about twelve swans that lived in the lake and that were to be seen going in and out of the castle. So she travelled on until she came to the castle and she saw the swans swimming in the lake. She went in to the castle, for nightfall was coming on, and she could not find any living person in it. But there was a big long table with twelve places set on it and twelve chairs drawn up to it, and in another room there were twelve beds all ready. Then she noticed that it was getting very dark, for the sun was after setting, and the next thing she knew was that twelve young men were coming into the castle. They found her inside.

'What will we do with this girl, for she has discovered our secret, that we are swans by day and in our own shape by night?' says one of them.

'We should kill her, of course,' says another, 'but it would be a great pity to kill such a beautiful girl.' They asked her who she was and she told them. And they were her twelve brothers under enchantment.

They entertained her well that night, and they spent the night talking. And when the morning came they turned back into swans. And the same evening, when they took their own shape again, one of them went off to a wise man that lived in the neighbourhood and told the wise man their trouble. And the wise man told them that there was a way to break the spell. It was not easy. The girl was to gather the *ceannabhán móna* and to spin it into thread, and to weave the thread into cloth and to make a shirt for each of the brothers from the cloth, and when that was done they only had to put on the shirts, and they would be in their own proper shape from that minute out. But from the minute she started to gather the *ceannabhán móna* she was not to say as much as one word to a human soul, or if she did, the spell would hold for ever.

The next morning she got up and got a big bag, and when

the swans flew away to the lake she set off on her travels, walking through every bog and mountain and filling the bag with the *ceannabhán móna*. And the people along her road thought she was a poor dumb woman, and they were kind to her, and gave her a place to sleep and a bite to eat. And when she had the big bag filled, she got the loan of a spinning wheel and started to spin it, and as soon as she had so much thread made, she wove a bit of cloth, and so on, all the time saying nothing until she would have enough cloth for the twelve shirts.

There was a prince in that part of the country, and he heard about the beautiful girl that could not talk, but that spent all her time spinning and weaving. And he came to see her, and he fell in love with her, because he thought there was no woman as beautiful in the whole world. And he asked her to marry him, and he told her she need do nothing except go on spinning and weaving if she wanted to. And she nodded her head to say that she would marry him. And so they were married and he took her away to his castle and gave her a fine room and a golden spinning wheel, and she spent all her days there spinning and weaving the *ceannabhán móna*. But the old hag that had put the brothers under the enchantment got to learn about her, and guessed what was up, and she made up her mind to stop her if she could. So when a baby was born to the new couple the old hag came in the night and stole the baby away, and she sprinkled a hen's blood on the cradle and the girl's nightdress, so that when the servants came in the morning they got a great fright and they ran down to the prince to tell him that it was how his wife had had the child killed during the night. And there was great confusion and questioning, and the poor girl was not able to say a word to show she was innocent, for fear of the spell. And they brought her to the court for killing her own child, and the judge gave the sentence, that she should be burned.

They put her in the prison, but they let her have her spinning wheel and her loom, and she was working day and night now, for she had eleven of the shirts finished and she was beginning the twelfth one. And the day came that she was to be burned, and they put her in a common car and drove through the streets to a place outside the town where there was a big pole standing up and a big heap of timber and turf around it to burn her. And all the time, when she was going in the car and when they were tying her to the pole, she was sewing away at the last shirt as fast as she could. And she had all the other shirts in a heap alongside her. Then the judge gave the order, and they lit the heap of turf and timber. The poor creature was distracted. 'Oh my brothers! Where are you?' says she, as loud as she could call.

And the next thing was that the people saw the twelve swans wheeling down out of the sky, scattering the fire with the wind of their wings. And all the swans stood in a ring around her and she commenced to throw a shirt over each one of them, and according as she did each swan was turning into a handsome young man. And when she came to the last one of them, the youngest brother, she had the shirt all finished except for one sleeve, and when he turned back into his own shape he had a swan's wing instead of his left hand.

Well, they told their story to the prince, how they were under enchantment, and how she saved them by making the shirts without saying a word, and how it was the old hag that had stolen away the infant. And the prince sent his soldiers to bring the old hag, and they found the baby still alive and brought the baby and the old hag back to the place where all the people were. And the judge said that the old hag was to be burned instead of the girl, and they threw her into the fire and burned her and that put an end to her capers. And the twelve young men went back to their own father and mother. And the girl was able to talk and laugh as much as she liked now, with her brothers saved and her fine husband and her lovely child. And they all lived happily ever after.

36: The Singing Bird

Once upon a time there was a king, and his wife, the queen died and left him with only one son. And after a while he was thinking of marrying again. And there was a queen over a neighbouring kingdom, and she was a widow with three young sons, about the same age as this king's son. And the king thought that if he married her, they could put the two kingdoms together into one, and that his young son would have the other king's sons of his own age to play with. So they got married, the king and the queen, and the king made no difference between his son and the queen's sons, but she was a bad and bitter woman, and she was always putting her own boys up to tricks against the king's son, to try to turn the king against him.

One time the three sons of the queen took a fine horse out of the stable, and drove him over a cliff. And that was the king's favourite horse, and his own son often asked for a loan of that horse to ride, but the old king would not let him, because the horse was so valuable. And the old queen was making up stories about the son, how he was seen taking the horse out of the stable and so on. But the son denied it and the king did not know what to believe.

And a short while after that the boys were out hunting together, and when the king's son got separated from the others, they killed the king's best greyhound, they stuck it with their swords. And when they came back to the castle, there was the searching and the questions, where was the greyhound? And it was known that it was the king's son that had taken the hound out that morning, and when the hound was found dead, it is he that is blamed for it, and the king was threatening to hunt him out of the kingdom entirely, and the old queen was delighted. But who should come up to the castle on horseback but a neighbouring gentleman and he had the true story for the king, for he was after seeing it all happening, and he passing through the wood. 'And if you look at your own son's hunting clothes you'll find no blood on them, but there should be blood on the other boys' clothes.' The king sent for the clothes, and sure enough it was as the gentleman said. And the king was not sure what to believe, between all the stories. But he called all the boys and he told them not to go out hunting again unless himself was along with them. 'And I'll keep my eyes open,' says he to himself, 'and I'll see whatever is to be seen.'

About a week after that they all went out hunting into the wood, and the king was watching all the time, and wondering all the time how he could put them to some sort of a test. And after a while, and they in the very middle of the wood they heard a bird beginning to sing. And never in all this world was the like of that song to be heard from any bird, it was so sweet and so musical. The king was very fond of music and he could forever hold listening to that bird, and he thought that if he had that bird singing to him every day in his castle he would live long and die happy. And he made up his mind that he would get that bird and test the boys at the same time. So he called them around him. 'Do you all hear that singing bird? Well, whichever one of the four of you will bring that bird alive and singing to me, I'll give him half of my kingdom now and the whole of it when I am dead.'

So, off with the four boys after the bird, and the bird flying from tree to tree, singing all the time, until in the end the bird went into a hole in a pile of rocks. And the four boys were poking around the pile of rocks, until they found a rock that they could move, and when they moved it they saw a big deep hole, just like a well, going down through the ground. It was very dark down in the hole, but they wanted to follow the bird, so they got a long rope, and then they drew lots to see who would go down. The first lot fell on the eldest son of the queen, and they lowered him down on the rope, but it was not long until they heard him shouting and bawling to pull him up. He told them that there was a man with a spear trying to stick him when he came down to the bottom of the well. So they drew lots again, and this time the lot fell on the second son of the queen, but he did no better; he was hardly at the bottom when he started to yell to pull him up, for the man with the spear was waiting to stick him below. And when the next lot fell on the queen's third son, he was not half way down when he was yelling to be pulled up out of the well again.

Finally the king's son went down. He didn't waste any time, but the minute his feet touched the bottom he made a drive at the man with the spear, to grapple with him. But the man with the spear only laughed. 'It is how I'm here to test the courage of anyone that comes down,' said he. 'The cowardly ones all go back up again. And you are the first man that had the courage to face me. And maybe I might be able to direct you to where you are going.' The son of the king told him his story, how he was trying to follow the singing bird, and the man with the spear told him that the singing bird was living in a castle a few miles away, herself and her father. 'And when you come to that castle, you'll be offered the height of hospitality. But you are not to eat a bite or drink a sup inside the walls of that castle. And I will give you the loan of my horse, and that will be a great help to you, but you have to be very careful of the horse.'

So the son of the king took the horse and he rode away to the castle, and he got a great welcome there. His horse was put in a stable and the table was spread with all kinds of food and drink before him. But he would not touch a bite or sup of it, but told the king his story, how he was searching for the singing bird. 'You are not the first one to come on that search,' says the king of the country under the ground, 'for the singing bird is my daughter. And maybe you will not be the last one either. For you must pass a test, and the man that passes that test can have my daughter to marry. You will have to go ahide for three days and I will search for you until I find you. And if I do not find you, I will go ahide for three days and you must look for me. And if I find you or you fail to find me you'll be put to death. But if I fail to find you and if you find me, you will marry my daughter.'

After a while the son of the king went out to the stable to see after his horse, to be sure that they were treating her right. And the next thing was that the horse spoke to him. 'It will not be long now until the king and his soldiers will be pulling the place down looking for you. And it will be hard for you to escape them unless you do what I say. What you are to do is to pull one hair out of my tail and go yourself into its place, and

107

the minute you try to do it you will take the shape of a hair of my tail.' And the next morning when he was supposed to go ahide, he did what the horse told him, and the king searched high and low and could not find a sign of him.

That same evening, when the king had the search given over, and the young man was back in his right shape again, he went out to tend the horse. And the horse said to him: 'You escaped well today, but you might not escape that way a second time. So what you will do tomorrow is to pull a tooth out of my lower jaw, and you go into the place of the tooth.' And so he did, and the old king held searching all day but he couldn't find a sign or a trace of him. And the third morning the horse had him warned to pull a nail out of one of the horse-shoes and go into the hole in place of it. And it failed the king to find him that day too.

Then it was the king's turn to go ahide. 'You bested me these past three days,' says he to the young man, 'however you did it. But you can be sure and certain that you won't find me when I go ahide on you. And then you'll pay for all the trouble you are after causing me these past three days,' says the king. So off he went ahide, and when the time came the young man searched high and low without finding a sign of him. Out with him to the stable with his heart in his boots, and told his story to the horse.

'Go out to the orchard,' says the horse, 'to the tree that is farthest from the gate. And pick the apple that is nearest the back wall of the orchard, and go to cut it with your knife.'

Out with him to the orchard, and found the apple and went to cut it. 'Hold your hand!' shouts the king, for he was hiding in the apple. 'You have me today,' says he, 'but it will be a different story tomorrow!'

The next morning, when the old king was gone ahide, the young man went straight out to the horse in the stable.

'Go in to the castle and get the loan of a gun,' says the horse, 'and go down to the lake and be aiming at the biggest drake that is swimming there with the ducks.' And so he did, and, sure enough, it was the king hiding in the shape of a duck.

'You have me again,' says the king. 'But however good you

are, I'll best you yet.'

The next day the old king went ahide again, and the boy went out to the stable for his instructions. 'Be in no hurry today,' says the horse, 'but spend the day making up to the daughter. And it won't come hard on you, because she is a fine, lovely girl. And persuade her to take you out for a walk all the day, looking at all her father's fine lands, and visiting her friends around the place. And when you come home in the evening, be sitting with her in front of the fire. And when you get the chance, take the enchanted ring off her finger, and be throwing it into the fire.'

And he gave the day walking and talking with the girl, and they got on well together.

And the same evening they were sitting in front of the fire, talking away. And when he got the chance he slipped the ring off her finger and was making to throw it into the fire. 'Hold your hand!' says the old king, coming out of his hiding place, for it was how he was inside under one of the jewels in the ring. 'That is an enchanted ring,' says the old king, 'and it is by magic in that ring that my daughter is able to take the shape of a singing bird. And now I must keep my bargain. Because it was how my daughter saw you in the wood when you were hunting with your father and your brothers, and it was how she led you here to the country under the ground. And I had to test you because many is the man that came looking for my daughter's hand in marriage, and only the best of men is good enough for my daughter. But you won the test, and now you can have her.' So they were married the next morning.

After a while, and all of them very satisfied with each other, the young man told his wife and her father about what was going on in his own country, how the stepmother was doing her best to turn his father against him. So the three of them set out for the young man's own country, and they explained everything to his father, all about the singing bird and the country underground. And the old queen who was the cause of all the trouble was sent back to her own castle and given strict orders to stay in it. And the young man and his wife would spend half of the year in his country and half of the year in her country.

And when the old kings died, they were the king and queen over the two countries.

STORIES FROM MICHAEL DAWSON

37: The Griffin

There was a very rich man living somewhere in the east of Ireland a long time ago. He had plenty of land. He had plenty of money. He had no shortage of anything except in his family, because his wife was dead and there was only the one daughter, and of course I need not tell you that he thought a lot of her. To listen to him talking you would think that the sun, moon and stars were shining out of her. And the two of them were living very happy in the place, but the father was very jealous of any young man making up to the daughter.

Well, one day the daughter got sick, and as time went on it was worse she was getting. She was so weak that she couldn't sit up in the bed. And the father had what doctors there were in the country brought to her, but not one of them had the right cure for whatever was ailing her. Until one day a travelling doctor, a sort of a quack, was passing the house, and he heard about the sick girl and the great pay that was to be given to the one that cured her. He went in and had one look at her. 'She is bad,' says he, 'but there is a cure for her. And that cure is three feathers out of a griffin's tail. And they must be plucked out of his tail; it will not do at all to pick up old ones off the ground. And there is only the one griffin living in this part of the world,' says he. 'And it is over at the other side of the River Suir he lives.'

Now this griffin was like a big bird, like a cock, but to have a man's head on him. And he was very savage, because the people used to be laughing at his appearance. And it was dangerous to go near him at all. And that was the reason the quack doctor mentioned the cure, because he was certain that no one would go next or near the griffin to ask for the cure. He knew that there was great healing in the feathers, but it was well known that the griffin was persecuted from people asking him for a feather, and that did not make his temper any softer.

Well, the news went out that the feathers were wanted, and there was this boy in the place, a poor farmer's son, and he said to himself that he might as well venture it. He sent word up to the big house that he was going for the feathers and to expect him back in a few days time, and away with him. He was travelling away and travelling away until the night was coming on and he called into a house on the side of the road. They gave him an invitation to be inside for the night and welcome. They were talking around the fire after supper, and he told them how he was going to the griffin.

'You'll have to be very careful of that griffin,' says the man of the house, 'and it would be better for you to go to his house while he is out. I hear that the wife is a good poor creature, and she would be more likely to help you. And while you are about it,' says he, 'will you ever find out what is wrong with my daughter. She is lying above in her bed this long while, and not a word or a stir out of her, although there is no appearance of sickness on her.'

He said he would.

The next day he travelled on, and coming on to the middle of the day he was getting hungry, and he turned in to a farmer's yard at the side of the road. They told him to draw up to the table and eat enough of whatever was going. And he told them where he was going, and the farmer gave him the same warning, to go to the door while himself was out, and make his request to the wife, for she would be more likely to help him. 'And while you are about it,' says he, 'maybe you would ask him where the key of my money box is. It is a very strong box, all iron and steel, and I can't get any good out of it, for the key is lost and I cannot open it by any manner or means.'

Jack said he would, and welcome.

Well, he travelled on, and coming on towards evening he came to the brink of the River Suir. And there was a boat there to carry the people across; there was no bridge there then, nor for long after that. And there was a man in the boat, going back and forward all day, taking the people across. And the man in the boat was greatly puzzled, for something was always keeping him in the boat, and he could not come out of it. Jack was going across in the boat, and, of course, he got into conversation with the boatman. He told him where he was going, to see the griffin and to try to get the cure. And the boatman warned him about the griffin. 'It would be better for you to watch him,' says he, 'for he is dangerous. But he has great knowledge. And by the same token, if you get the chance, will you ask him why I am not likely to leave this boat, night or day, and may the Lord spare you the health!'

Well and good. Jack promised faithfully to get the answer to that question, if he could at all.

He was travelling on and travelling on for a considerable time, until he came within sight of the griffin's castle. And it was late in the evening by this time, coming on to nightfall. And he saw this little woman coming out of the door of the castle, and he asked her about the griffin. 'He is my husband,' says the little woman, 'and he is not at home. He is not back generally until after the fall of dark. And I am greatly in dread for you,' says she, 'if he gets any sight of you, for he has a fierce temper, and he hates to see any strangers around the place. But if you tell me what you want from him, maybe I'll be able to get it for you, whatever it is. And I'll hide you,' says she, 'in the cupboard until he is gone again in the morning.'

So he told her about the three feathers and about the girl that was in the trance and the key that was lost and the man in the boat. And she said she would do her best for him.

So the griffin came home finally, and had his supper. And after a while they went to bed, and he fell asleep. And when he was asleep a while she pulled a feather out of his tail.

'What is this?' says he. 'Why have you woken me up?'

'It is like this,' says she, 'I was wondering why a girl would be stretched in bed in a trance, and not a word or a stir out of her?'

'I know of a girl like that,' says he, 'away over beyond the River Suir. And it is how she is under a spell. There is a lock of her hair stuck in a swallow's nest in the barn. And the minute that is put into her hand she will be as good as she ever was.' And he fell asleep again.

After a while she pulled the second feather. 'What ails you

113

now?' says the griffin, waking up.

'I was wondering,' says she, 'if there was a key lost on you, the key of the chest with all your money, where would you look for it?'

'I know of a man,' says the griffin, 'living over beyond the river. And if he only knew it, it is down through a crack in the floor of his own kitchen the key went, one day when it fell out of his pocket.' And he fell asleep again.

After another while she pulled the third feather. 'What ails you now?' says he, 'and why can't you let me sleep?'

'It is that man in the boat I am wondering about,' says she. 'Why is he always stuck in the boat?'

'It is that foolish man!' says he. 'Wouldn't it be easy for him to leave it, only to hand the oars to the next one that he is carrying across, and then he can leave it and the other man will have to stay in it. And now will you let me have my night's rest without pulling at me?' says he. And he fell asleep again.

All she did was to go over to the cupboard and let Jack out and hand him the three feathers. 'Did you hear it all?' says she.

'Faith I did, every single word,' says Jack.

'Be going now,' says she, 'and have a good piece of the road behind you by daybreak.'

Jack was on the brink of the River Suir by daybreak, and the boatman was there.

'What did he say about me?' says the boatman.

'Good news,' says Jack, 'and I'll tell it to you the minute I am landed on the other side.' He took him across.

'Now,' says Jack, 'all you have to do is to hand the next man the oars, and he will have to stay in it and you can go away.'

'Would you like to come over again to the other side?' says the boatman, 'and I'll charge you nothing!'

'Faith, and indeed I won't,' says Jack.

He travelled on until he came to the house of the man that had the key lost. And he told him what the griffin said, and they found the key, and the man was so pleased that he handed Jack the full of his pockets with gold out of the chest. And when he came to the next house, where the girl was in the trance, they found the lock of hair in the swallow's nest, and the minute it was put into her hand, up she jumped as lively as ever she was.

Finally he came to the house where the girl was sick. And the three feathers cured her. And nothing would do her father but that she would marry Jack. And they lived happily ever after.

38: Jack and the Friendly Animals

There was a poor widow-woman living in this part of the country long ago, and she had only the one son, and his name was Jack. They were very poor, and it was all the poor woman could do to keep the bite in their mouths when Jack was growing up. They lived in a lonely place, and Jack had no other child to be his comrade when he was small, and he always made friends of all the animals around the place, and he used to talk to them, and they used to talk to him, for in those times long ago, the animals could all talk like Christians.

Well, when Jack was about seventeen years of age he went to his mother one day and told her that it was time for him to go and seek his fortune. And the poor woman got his few things ready for him, a clean shirt and a pair of stockings and a little cake of bread for the journey. And this morning he put the things in a bundle and tied them to his stick, and off with him away to seek his fortune. When the dog and the cat saw him starting off, they ran after him.

'Wait, Jack,' says the dog, 'you surely won't go without us with you.'

'Come on and welcome,' says Jack. And off they went through a big wood that was on their road. They were not gone very far through the wood when they heard the sound of flying behind them.

'Wait, wait, Jack,' says the cock, 'surely you won't go without us.'

'Come on and welcome,' says Jack.

They came to a big green space like a field in the middle of the wood, and there was a big flock of goats grazing in the green space. And the biggest of them was an old puck-goat with mighty horns and a long grey beard. He came running over to Jack and his friends. 'Where are you off to, Jack?' says he.

'I am going to seek my fortune, and my friends here are coming with me.'

'Oh Jack,' says the puck-goat, 'am I not your friend too? And it is often I was thinking that I would go to seek my fortune. Can I come with you all?'

'Come on, and welcome,' says Jack.

They were travelling on and travelling on, until the night began to fall. And Jack was getting a bit in dread of the dark in the middle of the wood. And finally he said to the cat to climb up on top of a high tree and to see if there was any sign of a house to be seen. And the cat was up at the top of the tallest tree in the place before you could count ten. 'I see a light over there, but it seems to be far away,' says the cat. They settled to follow the light, and see if it was a house, and if it was a house to ask for a night's lodgings, and maybe a bite to eat for their supper. Every once in a while the cat ran up a tree, to keep track of the light, and in the end, and it coming on to the middle of the night, they came on this big house in the middle of the wood. There was light shining from the windows and the door was standing open, but there wasn't a single person to be seen.

Well, Jack and his friends went up to the door and knocked, and there was no answer. They knocked again, and called. The same thing, no answer. 'Come on,' says Jack, 'we'll go in and enquire if we can have the night's shelter.' In they went, but the house was empty. They went from one room to the next and up and down the stairs, but there wasn't a sinner to be seen. But there were riches of all kinds in the house, bags of gold and boxes of jewels and pearls and every kind of finery. And there was grand furniture, carpets on the floor and pictures on the wall, and a big table set for two people and as much food and drink on it as would be more than enough for ten. After calling and banging a lot, Jack says to his friends: 'It wouldn't be any harm for us to take a bite to eat,' and they all sat down to eat. There was soup and meat and bones, and bread and cakes, and bottles of wine and jars of whiskey, and they had a grand supper, for there was something there that every one of them could eat, meat for the cat and the dog, and bread for the cock and the gander, and the puck-goat ate as much as three of everything on the table, and swallowed a timber mug of whiskey and ate the timber mug as an after course.

Then it was time for them to go to bed for themselves. 'This is a fine bed for me,' says Jack, 'but where will the rest of you sleep?'

'Above on one of the rafters,' says the cock.

'Above in the loft,' says the gander.

'At the foot of your bed,' says the dog.

'On the pillow alongside your head,' says the cat.

'I'll stretch out on the settle,' says the puck-goat.

So they all settled themselves down for the night.

Now, this big house belonged to two robbers that were brothers, and every night they were travelling far away, robbing and plundering the castles and the rich people, and there is no knowing of the amount of wealth they had hid there around their house. And out in the night they were making for the house, coming home, with another big bag of plunder. And they noticed that the light was quenched. 'There must be someone in the house,' says one of them. 'Let you take your time here outside minding the road, for fear there would be more of them outside, and I'll steal in and see what is going on or who is interfering with our business.' And with that, in he creeps.

But you may be sure that Jack's friends heard him. The cat put his paw on Jack's ear and wakened him, and they all got ready for what was coming, only the puck-goat stretched out on the settle, snoring as loud as thunder. 'There you are, whoever you are,' says the robber, and he creeping over towards the settle, and a big sword in his hand. But the next thing was that the cat jumped up and stuck his claws in the robber's face, and at the same time the dog got a grip on his leg and knocked him. By the time he was able to struggle up the cock had his spurs on his hair and the gander was beating his face with the wings. And that was nothing until Jack joined in with the poker. And the worst of all was when the puck-goat woke up. 'Let you all stand back from him and give me room,' says the puck, taking

117

a run backwards to get room to charge. And with that he put the robber flying out through the front door into the yard, with every bone in his body broken. He managed to drag himself out to where the brother was. 'Oh, I'm dying,' says he, 'for the house is full of all sorts of devils, and they have me destroyed. There is one old devil of a woman and she stuck a sewing needle in my eye. And there is a blacksmith that caught my leg with his tongs. And another old hag who pulled the hair off of me, and another one that ruined my nose and my ears with wallops of her petticoat. And bad and all as that was it was not as bad as the man that pulled down a rafter and gave under me with it. But the worst of all was a giant that held all the time roaring like thunder and that stuck me with two spears and flung me out in the yard! And I'm dying now, with all the killing and tormenting I got from that pack of devils. And you had better run for your life, or they will be after you to murder you.'

So the first robber died and the second robber ran for his life through the country and never came near the house again, he was so much in dread of the pack of devils that was in it.

Jack and his friends all went back to sleep as soon as they were sure that the robbers were gone. And the next day Jack sent the dog and the cat back to his own house to bring the mother to the robbers' house. And they had gold, and silver and all kinds of riches, fine clothes and a feast laid on the table before them every day of the week. And Jack and his mother and all his friends lived contented in the robbers' house from that day to this.

39: The Feet-water

In every house in the country long ago the people of the house would wash their feet, the same as they do now and when you had your feet washed you should always throw out the water, because dirty water should never be kept inside the house during the night. The old people always said that a bad thing might come into the house if the feet-water was kept inside and not thrown out, and they always said, too, that when you were throwing the water out you should say *'Seachain!'* for fear that any poor soul or spirit might be in the way. But that is not here nor there, and I must be getting on with my story.

There was a widow-woman living a long time ago in the east of County Limerick in a lonely sort of a place, and one night when she and her daughter were going to bed, didn't they forget to throw out the feet-water. They weren't long in bed when the knock came to the door, and the voice outside said: 'Key, let us in!' Well, the widow-woman said nothing, and the daughter held her tongue as well. 'Key, let us in,' came the call again, and, faith! this time the key spoke up.

'I can't let you in, and I here tied to the post of the old woman's bed.'

'Feet-water, let us in!' says the voice, and with that, the tub of feet-water split and the water flowed around the kitchen, and the door opened and in came three men with bags of wool and three women with spinning wheels, and they sat down around the fire, and the men were taking tons of wool out of the bags, and the little women were spinning it into thread and the men putting the thread back into the bags. And this went on for a couple of hours and the widow-woman and the girl were nearly out of their minds with the fright. But the girl kept a splink of sense about her, and she remembered that there was a wise woman living not too far away, and down with her from the room to the kitchen, and she catches up a bucket.

'Ye'll be having a sup of tea, after all the work,' says she, as bold as brass, and out the door with her. They didn't help or hinder her. Off with her to the wise woman, and out with her story.

''Tis a bad case, and 'tis lucky you came to me,' says the wise woman, 'for you might travel far before you'd find one that would save you from them. They are not of this world, but I know where they are from. And this is what you must do,' and she told her what to do. Back with the girl and filled her bucket at the well, and back with her to the house. And just as she was coming over the stile, she flung down the bucket with a bang, and shouted out at the top of her voice: 'There is Sliabh na mBan all on fire!' And the minute they heard it, out with the strange men and women running east in the direction of the mountain. And in with the girl, and she made short work of throwing out the broken tub and putting the bolt and the bar on the door. And herself and her mother went back to bed for themselves.

It was not long until they heard the footsteps in the yard once more, and the voice outside calling out: 'Key, let us in!'

And the key answered back: 'I can't let you in. Amn't I after telling you that I'm tied to the post of the old woman's bed?'

'Feet-water, let us in!' says the voice.

'How can I?' says the feet-water, 'and I here on the ground under your feet!' They had every shout and every yell out of them with the dint of the rage, and they not able to get into the house. But it was idle for them. They had no power to get in when the feet-water was thrown out. And I tell you it was a long time again before the widow-woman or her daughter forgot to throw out the feet-water and tidy the house properly before they went to bed for themselves.

40: Tuppence and Thruppence

When I was a young fellow my Grandmother told me one day to go in to Kilfinane and to bring her out a half an ounce of snuff. She had a great liking for snuff, and she had not a single pinch left in the house. And so I had to go for it for her. Off with me along the road but I wasn't gone very far till I came to a field where the boys were hurling, and of course I joined them, and with the dint of the fun and the noise I forgot all about the snuff. It was dark when I came home, but instead of my supper it was a welt of a sally rod across the behind I got from the old woman, and strict orders to go back to the town at once for the snuff, and it now dark night, as black as pitch.

Well, off I went. What else could I do? And I was walking along the road when I heard the horse galloping away behind me, with the hoofs beating the road: 'Tuppence and thruppence! Tuppence and thruppence!' was the sound they were making. I shoved into the side of the road, for fear I would be trampled in the dark, and the horse passing me out. But he pulled over towards me; there was a man in the saddle.

'What are you doing out so late?' says he.

I told him about my Grandmother and the snuff.

'Climb up behind me and I'll give you a lift,' says he. Up with me behind him from the top of the road ditch.

The horse went like wildfire. So quick that you wouldn't believe it. The wind that was before him he could overtake and the wind that was behind him couldn't overtake him. We were miles away past the town before he stopped. I had no notion in what part of the country we were. And where were we but outside the gates of a churchyard. The rider said some word, and, God save the mark, didn't the gate of the churchyard swing open before us without anyone laying a hand to it. In with the horse, and the two of us up on his back.

'Hold my whip, now,' says he, 'for I have a bit of a message to do, myself.'

Down he jumps and starts rooting up a new grave. The next thing was that he had the corpse pulled up out of the grave, and thrown across the horse in front of me.

'Hold him tight,' says he, 'and for the life of you do not let him go!'

What else could I do but to take a hold of the dead man. But with the dint of the fright, didn't the whip fall from me. I was so much in dread that I hardly noticed it.

Up with him on the horse, and away with the three of us, myself and the stranger and the dead man, and we galloping 'Tuppence and thruppence! Tuppence and thruppence!' I thought that the whole country would be woken up by the noise of the hooves. It was not too long until we saw a light away out in front of us, and before long we were shoving near it. It was a great big house like a castle. An old woman came out to the door, with grey hair streeling down out of her head and a comb of teeth in her jaws like a hayrake. 'Oh, Mother of God!' says I, 'I'm done now entirely!'

He ordered me to come down off of the horse and give him

a hand with the corpse. The next thing he did was to handle a hatchet and cut the corpse up, the same way as you would cut up a pig, and to put about one half of it down in a big pot over the fire. He jointed the other half and put it down in a barrel in pickle like bacon.

It was not too long until the supper was ready. There was another pot and it full of fine russety potatoes. She put the potatoes out on the table, and she got three plates. 'Sit in now, men, let ye,' says she, 'and eat your enough.'

We pulled into the table. I was hungry enough and I was drawing a few of the fine russety potatoes towards me. But the next thing was that she made a drive at the pot with the flesh-fork and landed a big *plannc* of the dead man up in front of me on the plate. 'Eat up, now!' says the man. I was more in dread than ever, but as luck would have it there was a great big mastiff of a dog under the table, and every bit of the meat I cut, I gave it down to him, while I was doing great chewing on the russety potatoes.

Well, the supper was finished at last, and I was hoping to slip away. 'You are going,' says he.

'I am, indeed,' says I, 'for it is late for me to be out.'

'That is all right,' says he, 'but before you go, don't forget to give me the whip that I gave you to hold for me.' My heart sank down into my boots.

'It is in the churchyard where I let it fall and I holding the old man for you, sir,' says I.

'Go out and get it for me at once!' says he, 'and take good care to come straight back here with it!'

Off with me, as fast as I could take it from the legs. I reached the churchyard gate. 'Well now,' says I to myself, 'will I get the whip for him or will I make for home?' It was for home I decided to face, and you would hardly see me going, I was running so fast, taking every short cut across the fields, through hedges and briars. I was in sight of the house when what did I hear behind me, beating the road, but the 'Tuppence and thruppence! Tuppence and thruppence!' I let a yell out of me and made one mad leap in through the hedge and carried the door and the half-door in around the floor of the kitchen. With that the cock let a big crow out of him, for the dawn was just coming. Away with the horseman galloping like mad. I was gone off in a weakness, but I could hear the 'Tuppence and thruppence! Tuppence and thruppence!' fading away in the distance. I was safe, and I never heard tale nor tidings of the man or the horse from that day to this.

But it was no sympathy or compassion that my Grandmother gave me when she got me in the morning and found herself without the snuff, but the sally rod across the behind, and a strict order that I was to be back with the snuff within half an hour or I would not get a single bite for my breakfast!

NOTES

One of the most surprising things about Irish folktales is how widely many of them are told, not only in different parts of Ireland, but over wide areas of Europe and even of Asia. A good story, worth the telling, was retold again and again, and passed with great ease over linguistic boundaries, so that in many cases the same story was told in over forty or fifty languages in as many parts of the Old World. This became apparent to students of these matters during the nineteenth century, and much confusion among the seemingly endless stream of versions of tales resulted, until, in 1910, a Finnish scholar, Antti Aarne, produced a catalogue *Verzeichnis der Märchentypen (An Index of Folk Tale Types)* in which he listed a great number of tales told internationally and gave to each one of them a number by which it could be identified and have reference made to it. This great catalogue was revised and enlarged in 1928 by the American scholar Stith Thompson, who produced a further enlarged version, *The Types of the Folk Tale*, in 1961. This last work is now the guide of the student of folk tradition through the vast proliferation of tales which has resulted from the efforts of collectors to write down the old stories before they are forgotten. The student who sees a number such as 'Aa-Th. 1398' appended to the title of a tale knows at once that it is an international folk tale and that information about it can be found under this number in Aarne and Thompson's catalogue and in other reference lists; the stories in this present collection are so designated where they have been recognised as international tales.

Scholars in other countries have followed the lead of Aarne and Thompson by classifying the international folk tales known in their countries in accordance with the enumeration laid down by the two pioneers. Such lists have already been published from many areas. The Irish material has been brought to conformity by two experts in the field, Seán Ó Súilleabháin and the Norwegian scholar Reidar Christiansen; their joint work, *The Types of the Irish Folktale*, which analysed about 43,000 Irish tellings of international folk tales, was published in 1963. In this elaborate work interested people can find reference to the whereabouts of every known version of the international folk tales in Ireland.

Professor Stith Thompson carried the work of classification further in the international field when he published a large work in six volumes entitled *A Motif-Index of Folk Literature*, which gives a reference-number not merely to the general tale types but to every single incident or *motif*. I have however, deliberately refrained in the notes below from reference to this second catalogue, as being somewhat over-elaborate in a popular book of this kind.

1: The Boy who had no Story
This is a very popular tale in Ireland; *The Types of the Irish Folktale* enumerates nearly 140 versions of it. The horrible experiences of the man in search of a story vary considerably in different versions. Often it does not mention the search for a tale, but merely recounts ghastly adventures of the hero, as in the last story in this collection, no. 40 below. Ó Súilleabháin and Christiansen have adopted the number Aa-Th. 2412 B for this story.

2: The Spinning Woman

This is one of many Irish fairy tales which tell how a mortal helped the fairies and was rewarded for it.

3: The Buried Treasure

A hidden treasure over which some kind of supernatural protection has been set is a very common theme in Irish local stories. Here, as in many other places, tradition goes on to say that the treasure will be recovered only when monks of the same religious order return again to the old church. In other versions it belongs to the fairies, and it is they who still guard it.

4: The Three Wishes, Aa-Th. 750 A

A little international tale well known in Ireland.

5: The Gambler and the Hare

In Irish tradition the hare is a rather uncanny creature, for it may be a witch in disguise, as in story no. 23 below. There are other stories of gamblers playing cards with the Devil or with other strange opponents.

6: Carroll the Car Man, Aa-Th. cf. 1539 and 1542

A popular international folk tale theme is that of the seemingly simple fellow who outwits a mean or greedy person who sets out to cheat him.

7: The Servant Boy and the Farmer, Aa-Th. 1000-1002-1007-1006-1029

This is a very widespread international tale of which some hundreds of versions have been noted in Ireland; it is generally known as *The Anger Bargain*, and in different versions many different tricks are employed by the servant to anger the master.

8: The Wise Men of Muing an Chait, Aa-Th. 1291

This kind of tale, setting forth the silly doings of a family or of the people of some village or townland, is very common in Ireland and farther afield. Often it is told by the people of one district about those of another, while the foolish actions of the simpletons are very numerous in the various versions.

9: The Pious Man

The pharisaical attitude which renders apparently good deeds worthless in the sight of Heaven is a favourite subject of religious stories. This tale is told in Ireland sometimes of a man but more often of a woman. Ó Súilleabháin and Christiansen have given it the number Aa-Th. 1848* to distinguish it from the international tale in which a pebble is put in a box for each sin committed.

10: The Light of Heaven

This is one of many stories of virtuous persons wrongly accused of evil and shown to be innocent in some miraculous way.

11: The Blood of Adam

In West Limerick and North Kerry it was commonly said that the priest in this story was Father Patrick Ahern, parish priest of Athea, who was killed by a fall from his horse in the year 1804, an accident held to have been caused by the Good People in revenge for the bad tidings which he gave them. But it was told much more widely in Ireland, as proof that the fairies were not human.

12: The Coat on the Sunbeam
There are many such stories showing how virtue is made manifest and pride punished. Like many other religious tales it probably owed its popularity to its having been told as a pious parable by medieval preachers.

13: The Drink of Gold, Aa-Th. 1305 C
Several versions of this international tale are known in Ireland. In some the miser is a man, in others, as here, a woman.

14: The Pig-Headed Child
The awful consequences of speaking evilly of others, especially of the poor and helpless is another favourite theme of religious stories.

15: The Proud Girl, Aa-Th. cf. 1430
A version of the popular tale theme of 'castles in the air' or 'pride goes before a fall'.

16: Daniel O'Connell and the Cow
The clever pleading in court of Daniel O'Connell, the great Counsellor, is the subject of many stories. This one has a local connection, as Counsellor Thomas Goold, who had been a member of Grattan's Patriot Parliament and one of those who opposed the Union to the end, spent his later years as a resident landlord in Athea, County Limerick.

17: The Magic Fiddle
All over Ireland were tales of a musician who was given great skill by the fairies, and upon whose instrument nobody else could play. Most of them end in the same way, with the mysterious breaking of the instrument at the moment of his death.

18: Seán na Scuab, Aa-Th, 1383
In our area the scene of the elevation of the simpleton to high office was Limerick; in other districts other towns were singled out for the honour of having him as mayor.

19: The Fool and the Feather Mattress, Aa-Th. 1290 B*
This is another example of the simpleton story, see above.

20: The Fairy Path
The dangers inherent in interfering with the abodes of the Good People are set forth in many tales of this kind.

21: The Soup Stone, Aa-Th. 1548
Another example from the popular class of tales recounting how cunning cheats the simple but miserly.

22: The Snuff Box
There are many tales of this kind, of souls bound to the place of death until released by some human act. This version and the similar one which has the ghost smoking a pipe, are connected with the common Irish custom of saying a prayer for the dead when accepting a smoke or a pinch of snuff.

23: The Tailor and the Hare Woman
The witch in the shape of a hare is well known in Irish tradition; this story tells how the transformation was worked.

24: The Midnight Mass
One of the many tales about a ghost returning to earth to fulfil an obligation, but unable to do so without human help. In another well known Irish version the priest returns from the dead to destroy a dumb man's written confession.

25: The Prophecy, Aa-Th. 934
This story is told in many parts of Europe. Ó Súilleabháin and Christiansen list 116 Irish versions of it.

26: The Headless Coach
Signs and wonders presaging death are familiar in Irish tradition. They are, indeed, regarded as status symbols, as they are manifested only for the members of certain families of ancient and noble descent.

27: The Boy who had Knowledge
In another version of this tale which I heard in east County Limerick the storyteller, Seán Condon of Callan, Ballylanders, told it in the first person, as having happened to himself, and described how he, as the Clever Boy, got the man of the house to light a fire under the large boiler in which the interloper had hidden himself.

28: The Funeral Path
A local tale of a strange encounter at night.

29: The Coffin
Irish tradition abounds in stories of the abduction of humans by the fairies. Usually, as here, they are placed by the teller in his own experience, or in some particular named place, or told of named people. In some versions of the 'Girl in the Coffin' tale, she marries the young man who rescues her. Because of its resemblance to certain international types, this story has been given the number Aa-Th. 990* by Ó Súilleabháin and Christiansen.

30: The Brown-haired Boy, Aa-Th. 563-566
The poor boy setting out to seek his fortune and winning wealth and a bride with the help of magic objects is a well-loved folk tale theme all over the world. My father learned this version in Irish from his grandmother, but she may have got it from The Irish Fireside, 10/9/1883.

31: The World Underground, Aa-Th. 480
The World Underground – *An Domhan faoi Thalamh* – is one of those mysterious lands where the most wonderful things can happen in folk tales. A very similar version of this tale is in *The Irish Fireside* of 15/10/1883, and my great-grandmother's telling may owe something to this. But it is a well known and widespread Irish story.

32: The Tailor of Rathkeale, Aa-Th. 1640-1088-1049-1063 B
The weak and puny man who imagines himself a great warrior and slays giants by his cunning is a favourite figure of the folk tale. Hundreds of versions of this tale have been noted in Ireland.

33: King Whiskers, Aa-Th. 900
It is almost certain that my great-grandmother found this tale in *The Irish Fireside* of 12/11/1883. It has been recorded a number of times from oral telling in Ireland – Ó Súilleabháin and Christiansen note 11 instances of this, but it appears to have come into the Irish tradition from some printed source.

34: Máirín Rua, Aa-Th. 327-1119-480
This seems to have been borrowed directly by my great-grandmother from *The Irish Fireside* of 24/9/1883.

35: The Twelve Swans, Aa-Th. 451
My father knew this tale from his grandmother as *Léinte den Cheannabhán Móna*, 'The Shirts of Bog-cotton', and the old lady may have found it in *The Irish Fireside* of 13/8/1883, although the geese have become swans in her version.

36: The Singing Bird, Aa-Th. 301-550
Another adventure in the World Underground. My father called this story *Éan an Cheoil Bhinn*, 'The Bird of Sweet Music'; other versions of it are known from County Limerick, and it was a popular tale in many parts of Ireland.

37: The Griffin, Aa-Th. 461
The quest of three hairs from the monster's beard, or – as here – three feathers from his tail, and for the answers to difficult questions are often combined with other incidents to make a much longer tale than the simple version given here.

38: Jack and the Friendly Animals, Aa-Th. 130-210
This is a favourite story of parts of Europe, especially Germany, but not so commonly told in Ireland; it may have come into Irish tradition from some literary source, such as an early edition of *Grimms' Fairy Tales*.

39: The Feet-Water
Versions of this story are common in Ireland.

40: Tuppence and Thruppence
Another tale of strange adventures by night – see note to No. 1, above, told here in the first person as happening to the storyteller himself.